Copyright © 2012 by Shanika "Neek" Washington

All rights reserved. No part of this book may be reproduced, stored, or transmitted by any means—whether auditory, graphic, mechanical, or electronic—without written permission of both publisher and author, except in the case of brief excerpts used in critical articles and reviews. Unauthorized reproduction of any part of this work is illegal and is punishable by law.

First Edition

All characters in this book are fictitious, and any resemblance to real persons living or dead, is coincidental.

PUBLISHED BY

Printed in the United States of America

DEDICATION

This novel is dedicated to my beautiful children for whom I'd take my last breath. The day I gave life to each of you, is the day I found out what unconditional love was, there‘s nothing I wouldn‘t do for you all. Always remember no one loves you more than MAMA.

To Donald Washington a man that has shown me that there are still good men in the world. Don't stop ever loving me nor believing in me and I'll do the same.

And last but never least to the lovely ladies that are my first cousins but more like sisters Capresha Stevenson & Zakia Flint. I want to thank both you beautiful ladies for the inspiration and encouragement without you two, this novel wouldn't be in print today I love you deeply.

I LOVE YOU ALL THIS NOVEL IS FOR ALL OF YOU FROM ME.

ACKNOWLEDGEMENTS

First and foremost, I'd like to thank God for his mercy/grace without him none of this would be in ink today. I will be forever grateful.

To my parents E.Willis and Terry Flint I, I thank you both for two different reasons. Mother I thank you for introducing me to the Lord at an early age and installing all the wonderful qualities that I have now that has made me the strong, smart, and motivated mother and woman that I am today. Thanks mom, love you. Daddy I thank you for showing me REAL MEN take care of their children no matter what. You taught me my street smarts and how to throw some punches☺. Daddy I'll always remember your words "Daughter they're going to let your pretty face fool them and you're going to kick butt every time", Daddy you were right lol☺.

To my grandmother's Jessie and Alice, I thank you both for being strong women that are truly the backbone of your creation. When God blessed me with you two outspoken women as Grannies he blessed me with the best. You're loved and cherished.

To my brothers Antwon, Terry II, & Damien, I thank you for teaching me about video games, cars, and sports. Because, yes I'm very much a lady however I know how to hang with the fellas. FOREVER my brother's keeper. Much love always.

To my cousin Willie and my brother from another mother Kenshawn, I thank you both for allowing me to be a big sister in your lives and for truly being little brothers. Love you to men more than a kid loves Christmas!

To my Aunts Joyce and Kathy, I love you two ladies so much there's no word that can express how much I thank you two for everything, and cherish anything you ever given or taught me forever my ladies. Hugs and kisses☺.

To my Aunts Patricia, Leah, Ora (Bay), and Rosina, Merlynn and Chrissy, I just thank you all for being a wonderful group of Aunt's to me. I love each of you.

To my Uncles Tim, Martez, Corey and David, I thank you all for always having your niece back and looking out for me. You're appreciated greatly. Uncles Terry, Eugene, James, Cleveland, Houston and L.T. I love y'all too. Muah.

To my Father and Mother In-law Donald Sr. and Brenda, There are so many things I could say thank you for, however I'll just narrow it down to one. Thanks for always treating me like a blood daughter not just an in-law, but most of all thanks for being the best grandparents to my children. Love you both lots.

To a beautiful group of ladies, Monique Lopez, Tiffany Barmore, Tarsha Gulley, Doreece Edwards, Jimmetta Clark and Cynthia Young. I truly love each of you beautiful strong African American women. You all have played a major part in my life, each of you has shown me something different and I thank you not for being the first cousins that you are but for being the SISTERS I never had. Love you all dearly SMOOCHES☺.

To my circle of friends that are also beautiful women inside and out, Tenika Staton, Janel Mills, Shavonna Holmes, Lanea Williams and Mary Fretwell. I thank you ladies for the many years of trust, love and most of LOYALTY. You're appreciated greatly our friendships are cherished, KISSES.

To My Sister In-laws Charity &Carissa, I thank you for being outstanding sisters to me and amazing wives to my two brothers. But most of all I thank you along with a couple other ladies, Keisha and Sherry for my beautiful nieces and nephews, whom I love like they're my own. Tiara, Damien Jr., Marterrion, Shy, Cherish, Terry Armani, Dezzieon, Damarion, Tayvon, Taija, Serenity, and Antwon Jr. You are all TT's babies. HUGS and KISSES.

To De'Gyon, De'Breyon, Maki and Deterrace my four handsome God-children, I thank you boys for making me a very proud Godmother, with all your achievements, love you always and forever. "My Boys"☺

I also want to thank my guardian angels Aunt Glenda and Cousin Jeff for always watching over me protecting me. As I follow the path my life is leading me. I love you always and miss you both so much; however I know you're in good hands. Continue to Rest in Paradise my sweet angels.

To my Family and Friends, even if your name wasn't mentioned in print doesn't mean you're not loved nor does it mean I'm not thankful for you because I am. There's not enough ink or time for me to name each of you personally, just know you are all special to me. Charge it to my mind and not my heart. BLESSINGS!

In loving memory of my Great- Grandmother Mary (Mother) Sledge. R.I.P. 1911-2012- 101 Wonderful years!

Table Of Contents

Chapter 1

SINCERE IS HERE!

It was July 17th, 1975 and 105 degrees in Atlanta, GA. The hottest day of the summer and also the day Sincere Sunshine Simmons was born. Sincere was born to Neicy Taylor, a twenty-one year old, black law student and thirty-year old, Samuel Simmons, owner of Simmons and Simmons Luxury Car Dealership. They have been waiting for this day to arrive, even if the wedding wasn't for another six months.

"She is so beautiful," Sammy said, tired and overwhelmed.

"Neicy," as she glanced over at her happy future husband and their newborn baby girl.

"Yeah, Sammy she is, she's our blessing, our little sunshine," then she drifts into a sound sleep. As Neicy slept, Sammy, the proud father, held his precious baby girl and whispered, "Sincere Sunshine Simmons, the world is yours and daddy loves you." He said, sitting in his chair, rocking his baby to sleep.

Chapter 2

LIFE'S BEGINNING

August of 1992, life for seventeen year old Sincere was perfect. She was an only child. Her mom was Neicy Taylor Simmons, the biggest criminal lawyer in Atlanta, GA., and her father had developed his business into six Simmons and Simmons Luxury Car Dealerships. She was born with a silver spoon in her mouth; going to the best private school in Atlanta. She lived in an eight bedroom, six bathrooms, 4,905 sq. ft. mansion and wore nothing but the best designer clothes. Sincere woke up so excited this rainy August morning; one reason was because her favorite cousin Tyra was visiting from California. Tyra and Sin were close because they were both an only child and their fathers were brothers, which made it even better.

Tyra and Sammy's younger brother Steve moved to California after they opened a car dealership there. Business was good; therefore, it expanded to two dealerships very quickly.

Ding dong, the doorbell rang.

Sincere jumps off her bed and ran downstairs screaming, "I got it, I got it," pushing their housekeeper Mimi out the way. "Tyra" Sincere yelled, hugging her cousin tightly. "Wow, Tee you've grown since last year," Sincere chuckles, finally letting her go.

"Yeah, you have too," Tyra said, tapping Sincere's butt.

"Oh my gosh, you're finally here Tee, we have so much to talk about and only a week to do it, "as Sincere pulled Tyra up to her bedroom.

"So give me the tea and don't leave out the sugar," Sin said, to Tyra, while jumping on her bed, popping a few grapes in her mouth.

"Well," Tyra said, anxiously, "I'm officially a woman now!"

"What?" Sincere said, giving a blank stare, listening to what Tyra is saying to her, "We got our periods a long time ago, at thirteen years old."

Tyra laughed, "No silly, I lost my virginity! I'm no longer a virgin. I know we said, we would wait until marriage, but it just happened and I don't regret it!"

Sincere frowns, "Oh my gosh, Tee why didn't you call to give me this 411? I should have been the first to know."

Ugh, "Sin, don't be that way. I'm telling you now, plus everything happened so fast between me and Marques. We been like peas and carrots lately," Tyra said, smiling.

"Hmm, Marques the high school footballs star?" Sincere asked, popping more grapes into her mouth, smirking, "Peas and Carrots huh?" Sounds more like a plug and socket to me," Sin laughed, loudly stating, "I forgive you this time," she said, throwing a pillow at Tyra.

The girls laughed and talked for hours.

Sincere looked up at her clock, it was 1:45am.

"Whew, Tee its almost 2 am, have we really been catching up this long? Wow, time flies when you're having fun, talking about old times, I guess."

Let's get a midnight snack," Sincere said, grabbing Tyra's arm, as they headed down to the kitchen. When they reached the hallway, they noticed the kitchen light was on. In the kitchen was Sincere's mom, Neicy, at the table with her favorite bottle of wine, half gone, but still pouring.

"Hey, my two favorite girls," Neicy said, looking up from her glass.

"Hey Ma,"

“Hey Aunt Neicy,” the girls replied, in unison.

“What are you still doing up? Sin asked her mother, as she grabbed a few things out the fridge to make turkey sandwiches.

“Oh, I'm just thinking baby,” Neicy said, still sipping wine.

“About what,” Sin asked, as she poured mayo on a slice of bread?

“Well baby girl, momma got some news today; I haven’t told your father because I'm not sure what I’m going do about it, although, I know he will be more than thrilled about this news.” “What mom, what is it?” Sincere asked anxiously, as she scooted a plate over to her mom, while looking at her favorite cousin to hear what she had to say.

“I'm 9 weeks pregnant,” Neicy said, sadly.

Sincere screamed loudly, overjoyed, “Oh, momma that's good news! I've been waiting for a little brother or sister for many years now.”

“Yeah baby girl I know, so had your father. I'm just not sure another baby is what I want right now in my life. My career is at its peak, I'm the most prestigious black female criminal attorney in Atlanta, and that's a major accomplishment for me.” Neicy said, as she grabbed her daughter’s hand, looking into her eyes!!!!

Sincere softly squeezed her mother’s hand and asked, “So, what are you going to tell daddy?” “Baby girl, I'm going to have a talk with your father when he gets home tomorrow, after his flight lands at noon. We will have a nice lunch and I'll give him the news then.”

Sincere and Neicy hugged.

Chapter 3

GETTING OUT

The sun beamed through the blinds on Sincere and Tyra's faces. Sincere stretched, looking over at tired and still sleeping Tyra, and then notices the time on the clock showed 2:15pm. She jumped up quickly and went into her bathroom to get herself together. She ran her hands through her hair and then rushed downstairs to where she knew her father would be conversing with her mother. As Sincere reached the dining room, she saw only her father Sammy smiling and sipping on his favorite brand of cognac. Sammy noticed his precious daughter entering the room and gave her a big hug, kissing her on the forehead.

"Hey sweetheart, did your mother tell you we're pregnant?"

"Yes daddy she did," Sincere said, hugging her father tightly and smiling.

"So pumpkin, how do you feel about having a new addition to our family?" Sammy asked Sincere with concern. "Oh daddy, no need to look concerned, I'm happy I'll have a little sister or brother. It's something I've been wanting for a long time now." Sincere smiled! "Where's mom?" Sincere asked her father, looking around their huge black marble kitchen.

"She's taking a nap baby girl. She said, you guys stayed up late last night."

"Yeah we did dad," Sincere said, as she fixed her lunch their housekeeper Mimi prepared which looked so good.

Mimi had been with the family for seventeen years

now. Actually, she was her parent's housekeeper shortly before Sincere was even born. So Sincere loved Mimi like a second mom. Sincere sat down to eat her lunch and Mimi said, to her as she cleaned up the kitchen, "So Sunshine, what' your plan for today with Tyra?" "I don't know," Sincere said, as she shrugged her shoulders. "We will probably hit up Lenox Mall and do some shopping, spending daddy's money." Sincere chuckled, taking a bite of the chicken almond salad that Mimi prepared.

As Sincere finished her salad, Tyra came strolling in, rubbing her eyes, "Afternoon Sin and Mimi." She asked, Sin, "Why didn't you wake me?"

"Tee you looked so peaceful, I didn't want to bother you, but hurry up and get a bite to eat while I get dress. We got a big day ahead of us!" Sincere said, rubbing Tyra's shoulders and as she headed towards her bedroom to get ready.

It was 4:30 p.m. ! Sincere and her cousin, Tyra finally were ready to hit Lenox Mall.

"How do I look"? Sincere asked Tyra.

"You know you look cute cousin, why do you even ask?" Tyra looked at Sincere, a seventeen year old, five foot eight, green eyed, black and Creole beauty with caramel brown skin, almond shaped eyes, long curly hair extending down her back, with a body that had a lot of potential. "Thanks Tee. You're stepping out looking like Barbie herself." Sincere playfully winked at Tyra, aka Tee, who's also seventeen years old, five foot nine, hazel green eyes, Black and Creole, honey brown skin, big bright bold round eyes with curly chin length hair. She also had a body with much potential. The girls headed downstairs.

Sincere wore Prada, head to toe, from her shades to her sandals. Tyra, wore Fendi, also from head to toe; both ladies looked like models as they hopped into Sammy's 1992 Bentley where his driver, Charles aka Chuckie D waited to drive them to Lenox Mall.

As they got closer to the mall, Sincere asked Tee, “So whatcha want to do tonight?”

Shay had invited us to a party tonight at Keyvon Millhouse’s mansion in Huntley Hills. Keyvon Millhouse? Tyra smiled, giving Sincere that look. “Mm, huh?” Sincere laughed. Huntley Hills was where the richest of the rich lived and all the homes were over two million dollars and up. It was where the parents are too busy traveling or working, so their kids are left with housekeepers and nannies, which were like leaving them, home alone. So of course the kids get buck wild and throw lots of parties, where there's plenty of food and alcohol, lots of pot smoking and sex if the chance was given.

The girls are still giggling, as they pulled up to Lenox Mall.

“This is bananas! There’s nowhere to park,” Sincere said, frustrated and then told Chuckie D that he can leave and they'll give him a call him on the car phone from a payphone when they were ready to leave.

So Chuckie dropped the girls off in front of the mall and they jumped out and headed inside. The girls were headed to the Coach store when they happened to see seventeen year old Keyvon Millhouse, his brother, eighteen year old Keithen, and twenty year old Tavarious Campbell.

“Oh my gosh,” Tyra squeezed Sincere’s hand saying; “There goes Keyvon. Girl, I'm about to melt.”

Well don't melt, just stay cool! Remember, we're Simmons and we never get nervous,” Sincere told Tyra, as she squeezed her hand back.

“What's up Sin?” Keyvon said, as they passed each other.

“What's up Keke?” Sin replied back, with a smile.

“I know y'all coming to our party tonight at my

parents crib?" Keyvon said, with confidence.

"Umm, maybe," Sincere laughed loudly.

"We'll be there," Tyra said, quickly, before Sincere could say anything else.

"Cool, see you ladies tonight," Keke said, as he and his guys left the mall.

"Oh my God; Sin we have to get some fly outfits for the party tonight. No doubt, everyone who's anyone will be at this mansion party; the football and basketball teams, the most popular teams in Buckhead, Yaaaaay! We are in there like swim wear," Tyra high-fived Sin.

Sincere gave Tee that look, "Umm, I usually don't attend wild parties, but I'll go this time, only for you though Tee, but we're not staying long ok?"

"Okay we'll only be there an hour tops," Tyra smiled, doing her happy dance.

Chapter 4

DADDY'S GIRL

"Ooh my bed; an exhausted Sincere said, throwing her bags on the floor and diving onto her bed. "No Sin! No time for naps, it's a party in Huntley Hills tonight with our names on it, get up and call Shay and let's get ready."

Tyra put the phone on the bed for Sincere to call Shay.

"Ugh," Sincere said, pulling herself up from her king-sized canopy bed to call her bff.

"Hello," Shay answered.

"What's up, Shay this is Sincere. I'm calling to see if you're still going to Keke's party tonight? Because me and Tee want to roll with you?"

Shay replied, "Shoot yeah, I'm going. I'll be at your house in 45 minutes."

Sincere hung up the phone to start getting ready before Shay arrived.

An hour passed and the girls weren't ready yet. When Shay walked into Sin's room she said, "Can you two ever be ready on time? I'm twenty minutes late!

Sincere laughed, "We're almost ready," spraying her hair with water to make it curlier.

"Aye, why didn't I get the memo we were wearing Coach tonight?" Shay said, as she eyeballed Sincere and Tyra, dressed in their matching Coach romper's and sandals.

"Aw, it was a last minute decision girly," Tyra answered, as she glossed her lips.

"Uh, huh," Shay pouted, putting her keys in her Louis Vuitton bag.

Shay was 5'9 with mocha skin; dark brown bedroom eyes with a short Halle Berry haircut. Unlike Sin and Tee, Shay's body shape was perfectly thick in all the right places. She was an eighteen year old hood girl, originally from Southeast Atlanta whose father became a millionaire overnight by purchasing twenty dollars worth of lottery tickets that made him forty-five million dollars richer.

Sincere and Shay met two years ago when Shay's parents moved a few houses down from them, after her father's big win.

"Okay, you ladies should be ready by now," Shay said, popping a piece of gum in her mouth.

"Yep, we're ready," the girls said, in unison, as they headed down to Shay's car.

"Hey, hey, where are you young ladies going this evening?" Sammy said, as he looked up from some business papers.

"We're going to a back-to-school party in Huntley Hills at the Millhouse's, Daddy." Sincere rushed to hug her dad and get her kiss on the forehead, before he asked anymore questions.

"Okay sweetheart, you girls have fun, be safe and make sure you're home by midnight." Sammy said, sipping his drink and returning to his paperwork.

Walking to her 91' Volkswagen bug, Shay said, "I can't wait to get to this party, everyone is going to be there."

"Tee, said, I can't either. I thought she was going to have a heart attack today in the mall when we saw Keke."

Sincere laughed, putting on her seatbelt. On the drive to the party, the young ladies were still glossing lips and fixing hair. When they finally pulled up to the Millhouse's mansion there were cars everywhere; kids hanging outside and the music was blasting.

"Yep, we're here and it's bananas at the Millhouse's tonight. I thought our mansion was big, but this one is two of ours.

"Whoa, I like it," Sincere said, as they walked up the driveway to the door. Before they could ring the bell, a drunken Keke opened the door, with a joint dangling from his mouth.

"Come in ladies, come in and welcome to the Millhouse Manor," as the young ladies walked through the door, Sincere whispered, "We're sticking together tonight; we're not splitting up, got it girls?"

Tyra and Shay both nodded, as they walked into the Millhouse's five million dollar mansion, which was immaculate, by the way.

The music blasted and the crowd ranged from ages fifteen to twenty-one years old. The party was live yet wild and not what Sincere was used to. However, she decided to make the best of it in order to make her cousin Tee happy.

"You ladies want a drink?" Keke offered, reaching for a huge bottle of cognac off the counter.

"Sure why not," Tyra said, nudging Sincere to take the drink.

The ladies got their drinks and then moved through the smoked-filled mansion, looking for Shay, who obviously forgot they were supposed to be sticking together. As they walked onto the patio toward the pool, they saw Shay, smoking a joint and talking to Skeeter Johnson.

Skeeter is Keke's first cousin and a sophomore at Harvard who was visiting home for the summer.

"Hey college man," Sincere said to Skeeter, sipping her drink while sitting on a cushioned patio chair.

"What's up Miss Sincere Simmons?" Does your dad

know his little princess is at a house party where everyone is running wild?" Skeeter asked, laughing and reaching to give Sin a hug.

"Aw, I see you got jokes Skeet and your last name is Murphy now right, like… Eddie Murphy, get it?" Sincere replied, giggling and hugging Skeeter back.

"Aye Skeet, you remember my cousin, Tyra, don't you?" Sincere asked, pointing to Tyra, who stood there fully focused on Keke by the pool.

"Uhm yeah, your Uncle Steve's daughter," He reached out to shake Tyra's hand.

"So Skeet, how much longer you here? " Shay asked, licking the top of her cup.

"Kevin and I leave tomorrow night baby. We got things shaking back at home," Skeet grabbed Shay to hug her.

"Do you mean Kevin, Keke and Keithen's older brother ? " Shay asked.

Yeah, he said, kissing Shay on the cheek.

"Hey, don't get fresh with me Skeeter, she said, with a little smirk.

"Don't worry I won't do anything you don't approve of baby," he said, smirking back.

As they laughed, smoking joints and remembering old times, twenty-one year old Kevin Millhouse walked up with a big smile, holding a cup of cognac in his hand. Kevin was Keke and Keithens half-brother that their father had from a previous relationship.

Kevin pulled up a chair next to Sincere and asked, "What are you guys out here talking about? " "You," Sincere said, laughing and nudging Kevin.

"Oh yeah," Kevin said, nudging Sincere back as they laugh. "Sin, you're looking really nice tonight, Kevin whispered in her ear.

“Why thank you, Kev. I just threw this outfit together,” She said, smiling slightly at Kevin. “Well I'd love to see you when you've taken your time, if this is what you call thrown together.” Kevin rubbed Sincere’s arm. She smiled again while pulling away slowly from Kevin.

A few minutes went by and Shay said, “Hey Sin and Tee, I'm going to get another drink you ladies want one,” pulling Skeeter towards the house with her?

As Sincere fixed Tee's romper strap, Keke walked over smiling. She grabbed Tyra’s hand, “Can I talk to you for a minute Tee?”

Tyra replied, “Yes,” very calmly. All the while, on the inside she screamed and jumped with excitement. She was so in love with Keyvon “KeKe” Millhouse, without him even knowing it, but he would soon find out how Tyra felt about him. She looked tipsy.

Sincere said, “I'll be right back,” ordering her not to leave that spot. Sincere threw her hands up nodding her head in agreement. She continued enjoying her drink, as she waited for either Tee or Shay to return.

Kevin moved a little closer to Sincere, asking, “Would you like to take a walk with me?” he held out his hand for Sincere to walk with him.

With much anxiety and hesitation, she grabbed Kevin Millhouse’s hand while thinking to herself; *he is so fine*, but also, four years older than her. They walked at a slow pace, as he showed her the outside grounds of his father's estate. They came to a huge oak tree that sat far back, away from the house and the party.

Kevin took off his jacket, placed it on the ground, then told Sincere to sit down on it and relax. She hesitated, but decided to honor his request. Kevin lay next to her. They sat there talking, laughing and enjoying each other. All of a sudden, Kevin gently grabbed Sincere’s face and kissed her soft, glossed lips.

Sincere pulled back and said, "Kevin, I'm not ready for this yet, I'm still a virgin."

"Aah baby, don't worry about that," Kevin reassuringly said, as he's kissed and pushed his body against hers Sincere nervously pushed him off of her, "Kevin I think we should go back to the party. I'm sure Tee and Shay are looking for me!"

Kevin aggressively continued to kiss and rub on Sincere's shaking body. He said, "Oh baby, wait they're not gonna leave without you, aren't you enjoying this?"

Sincere's nervousness had turned to down-right fear. She pushed Kevin away and said, "No Kevin, stop! I told you I'm not ready for this, I'm still a virgin!"

Kevin said, "Come on Sincere baby, don't be that way, you know you want this. I'll be gentle baby girl, I promise, all the time pulling down her romper.

"No, Kevin No, I said, No! Now stop it!"

Kevin became angry and slapped Sincere across her cheek and said, "Shut Up!"

Sincere wanted to stop acting like a scared baby. She was uncontrollably shaking and crying for two reasons; first, she'd never been slapped before, by anyone, and secondly, Kevin Millhouse was forcing himself on her.

"Ooh, Sincere baby, you feel so good, "He whispered, as he pushed his penis in and out of her tight vagina.

Sincere was scared. She laid there in complete shock, while crying and in so much pain as Kevin Millhouse had his way with her body. As Sincere laid there on the ground, her mind and body was paralyzed in disbelief about what just happened, her virginity was just taken, against her own free will. She felt so violated and nasty, but most of all, she felt she was no longer Daddy's little girl. She never imagined, in a million years that this would be how her first time having sex would be.

Sincere pulled herself off the ground and brushed the grass from her clothes. She walked back to the house where everyone was still partying. She shivered and cried as pain ravaged throughout her body, and her clothes were in shambles. Sin reached into her purse and grabbed her mirror. She then wiped her tears and cleaned the blood from her lip. As she reached the pool area, she saw Tyra and Shay talking to Keke and Skeeter.

"Girl, where have you been, we've been looking all over for you," Shay said, pulling Sin close to them?

"I must have dozed off from drinking that liquor. I'm tired, can we go now please," Sincere said, as she walked towards the door to exit.

As they approached the car, Sin said, to Tyra, "You two ride shot gun, I need to chill in the back."

"Ok cool," Tyra replied, jumping into the passenger seat of Shay's bug.

The ride home was pretty much a daze to Sincere. She couldn't wrap her mind around the fact that she had just been raped, by Kevin Millhouse.

They pulled up to Sincere's house, Shay said, I'm spending the night bitches, so one of you are making room for me in one of those beds."

"You can have my bed Shay; I'm not doing much sleeping tonight. Sincere pulled out her keys to open her house door.

When they entered Sin's room, Tyra and Shay instantly raved about their night. Sincere went straight to the bathroom and turned on the shower. She took her clothes off and noticed blood stains in her panties. Tears rolled down her face, as she attempted to scrub her body clean. The more she scrubbed the more dirty she felt. Her first time was not what she thought it would be. It was not a priceless moment shared by two people in love; it was rape;

her purity snatched from her.

Sincere walked out of the bathroom with her hair still dripping wet. She grabbed a towel to dry off while still listening to the girls talk about how much fun they had.

"So Sin, where did you disappear to? We searched all over that mansion. Where were you?" Shay probed.

Tears flowed from Sincere's pretty green eyes, as she said; I'd rather not talk about it! I want to forget it ever happened.

What happened? Shay and Tyra drew more closely to Sincere, who cried uncontrollably because she was distraught.

Sincere fell onto her favorite cousin's shoulders, hysterical.

"Sin, what happened, what's wrong? " Tyra asked, hugging her cousin tightly.

"Oh Tee Kevin raped me, Kevin Millhouse raped me!" Sincere screamed out.

"What?" Tyra said in total shock.

"Oh hell naw! That nigga gots to get dealt with," Shay said, jumping up, reaching for Sincere's lip shaped phone.

"No!" Sincere ran towards her upset best friend, before she could make any phone calls.

"Huh, what do you mean? Sin fuck that! That nigga raped you, he took something from you, and you can't get it back," Shay said, snatching the phone back from Sincere.

Sincere unplugged her phone and said, "No Shay, I don't want anyone to know; besides, the Millhouse name is powerful in Atlanta. I know my daddy has money and power here too, but we don't need this kind of shit getting out. Then I become everyone's pity party.

Sincere grabbed Shay and Tyra hands and begged,

“Promise me what happened to me tonight, it stay’s here, between us three and never brought up again. They agreed, “Promise”.

Chapter 5

BAD NEWS

It was October 1992 and Sincere was a senior at one of the best private schools in Georgia. She decided to move forward with her plan of having a great senior year, forgetting about the awful mishaps in August.

"Momma you look beautiful this morning," Sincere said, rubbing her mother's four months pregnant belly.

"Thanks baby girl, I can't wait until it's over," stuffing the rest of her bagel in her mouth. Sincere opened the pantry to grab her favorite cereal she hadn't eaten in years, Fruity Pebbles. As she made her bowl of cereal, Mimi walked in, "Morning Sunshine, Fruity Pebbles, I haven't seen you eat these in years.

"I take it you missed them," Mimi chuckled and began making Mr. Simmons' coffee before he made his way downstairs.

"Yeah I had a taste for them, and they are so good." Sincere gulped a spoonful of her cereal. She finished eating and then hurried up to her room to get dressed for school.

"Hmm, what should I wear today?" Sincere said, to herself, looking through her closet of designer clothes. Friday was casual day at school, no uniforms, so she always brought out her best. As she dressed, she felt light headed.

Ooh, I should sit down for a moment, she thought to herself. As she sat there, she wondered why she felt light headed all of a sudden.

While she pondered, she heard a car horn, "*Beep beep*," she looked out of her room window and saw Shay and yelled, "I'm coming, stop honking your horn."

Sincere ran down the stairs to get in the car. They headed off to school.

"Umm, it's about time slow poke," Shay said, pulling out of the driveway. They pulled up to the parking lot of Belhaven Private School.

Sincere said, "Ugh girl, I'm not ready for Mrs. Jones Algebra test today." "Me either, but oh well," Shay laughed.

As the girls got out of the car, Sincere suddenly felt light headed again, this time throwing up. Ugh, gross Sin, what did you eat this morning," Shay asked, searching for a napkin in her Louie Vuitton purse?

"Nothing, just some cereal," Sincere said, wiping the vomit from her mouth. "I've been feeling real crazy lately girl and I don't know what's wrong." Sincere looked at her best friend confused and worried, but most of all scared.

"Do you think you're pregnant?" Shay asked nervously, opening the car door for Sincere to get back in.

Sincere laid her head back on the seat of the car, "Oh my God Shay, what if I am pregnant?" I've been so busy blocking what Kevin did to me out my mind. I guess I didn't realize my period hadn't come yet."

Sincere's body shook. She was nervous and tears rolled down her face.

"Shay, I can't have Kevin Millhouse's baby. Then I'd have to tell everyone what he did to me that night and I really want to forget it ever happened." Sincere cried harder than before. "Well friend, it's only one way we're going to find out." Shay said, pulling out of the school parking lot.

They pulled up to a clinic. Sincere read the sign, *Piedmont Woman's Health Center.*

"Whoa, wait a minute, why are we here?" Sin asked, anxiously.

"Girl chill out, this is where we're going to find out if

you're knocked up without your parents finding out," Shay said, opening the car door for Sincere to get out the car so they could go inside and hear the potential damage. There was no doubt in Shay's mind Kevin Millhouse's trifling ass had gotten her best friend pregnant. However, she would wait for the results.

"How may I help? " the receptionist behind the desk asked Sincere and Shay, as they approached the desk.

"Yes, she would like to take a pregnancy test," Shay said quickly, before Sincere could even get a word out.

"Ok honey, fill out these papers and bring them back when you're finished. A doctor will see you shortly." The receptionist handed Sincere a clipboard with papers and a pen connected to it. "I'm so nervous my hands are sweating and shaking. I can't fill out these papers. I can't even think straight." Sincere said, giving the clipboard to Shay.

"Aww hell Sin, I'll fill the papers out, you just put your John Hancock at the end, deal?" Sincere nodded, "Yeah deal."

"Sincere Simmons, the Dr. will see you now."

Sincere grabbed Shay's arm, urging her to get up and go with her.

"Hi my name is Lisa; I'm Dr. Washington's nurse. I'm going to ask you to give me a urine sample in this cup and then ask you a few questions."

The nurse smiled nicely and handed Sincere a small cup showing her to the restroom. She came out more nervous than when she went in. Sincere handed the nurse her small cup and they walked into an empty room.

"Okay Sincere, I have to ask you a few questions, weigh you, take your blood pressure, and then Dr. Washington will be in to see you shortly.

While waiting for the doctor to enter, Sincere looked at Shay and said, "I'm not having this baby, Shay, I just can't. I refuse to have a baby by a man that raped me. I wouldn't be able to look at my child, and it would be too much pain for me."

"Girl no one gave us results yet, calm down, we're wishing for the best. Chill out!" Shay rubbed her best friend to calm her down. When in reality, Shay was just as worried as Sincere, because nine times out of ten, Kevin Millhouse had gotten her friend pregnant against her will.

"*Tap tap*," there was a knock at the door. A short petite black lady with shoulder length hair walked in.

"Hi I'm Dr. Washington. Which one of you is Sincere?" she asked, shaking both girls' hands. "I am," Sincere answered.

"Well, do you want the good news first or the bad news?" Dr. Washington asked, glancing over Sincere's chart.

"Give me the good news first," Sincere said, "How about the bad news first, then I'll give you the good news," Dr. Washington suggested. "Well Sincere, you are pregnant. That's bad news at seventeen years old. However, the good news is you are between six and eight weeks, so there's time to terminate the pregnancy. Also, keeping your unborn child or adoption are options too. I don't know your situation, but here are some pamphlets and my card; whatever your decision, I am here to help you." Dr. Washington handed the pamphlets and her card to Sincere and walked out of the room.

As they walked through the double doors of the clinic, Sincere's mind spun, like a merry-go- round.

With all of the thoughts swinging through it, Sincere yelled, "Wait Shay! I have to make an appointment to end this pregnancy. I refuse to be pregnant by a twenty-one year old man who raped me."

The girls turned around and went back inside the

clinic.

"Back so soon," the receptionist asked, smiling, asking Sincere, "How may I help you, again?" Sincere leaned closer to the desk, whispering, "I'd like to make an appointment to end a pregnancy."

"Aww honey, that's nothing to be ashamed of, how soon do you need the appointment? She said, looking up available appointments.

"Soon as possible," Sincere replied.

"Okay, we have 10am, Saturday, November 4th . The cost is four hundred and twenty five dollars. Make sure not to eat anything the night before you arrive." she explained, handing Sincere a slip of paper.

Sincere looked at the paper and said, "Great I'll be here, see you guys then."

The ride back to Shay's house was silent; neither of the girls said anything. Pulling into Shay's driveway, Sincere felt nauseous again.

"This crap is for the birds," she said, dragging herself to Shay's front door. Sincere ran up to Shay's room, into her bathroom, throwing up again. This time it went on for 15 minutes.

"Ugh," Sincere said, exhausted, walking out of the bathroom. "Oh God, November 4th needs to hurry up and get here. I feel like I'm dying. I should find Kevin Millhouse and give him a taste of his own medicine for doing this to me."

"I told you we could have had my cousin Tip from Decatur deal with that nigga back in August." "Sin, it's no point in crying over spilled milk now; you know what you got to do, so do it! I'll be here for you; that's what friends are for."

Shay smiled, handing Sincere a blanket so she could get some much needed rest, after their long morning.

"Wake up girl, school will be out soon," Shay tapped Sincere, lightly, waking her up.

"Wow! Its 3pm already, we better get rolling so you can get me home?"

Sincere got up and walked into the bathroom to freshen up to go home as if she spent the day at school. They left.

"How was your day sweetheart?" Sammy asked his precious daughter.

"It was just another boring school day daddy."

She reached out to hug her father and to receive her usual kiss on the forehead.

"Where's mom and Mimi?" she asked, heading to the kitchen.

"They're out shopping baby girl," he answered, sipping his Cognac and walking toward his office on the west wing of their mansion.

Sincere was still tired and very hungry. She made herself a roast beef, turkey and ham sandwich. She knew her body was changing, because she never ate as much as she'd been eating lately.

Yep, I'm knocked up; Sincere thought to herself, as she took a big bite of her sandwich, stuffing a few chips in her mouth at the same time. She headed to her room to finish her sandwich, just in case her mother and Mimi returned from shopping; she couldn't let them see how her appetite had picked up.

As she lay on her bed, devouring her sandwich, Sincere thought to herself, "*I have a small person growing inside me, a blessing to most, because couples try every day to make a baby.*" But not in seventeen year old Sincere's case, she thought of it as a curse. She was raped and violated by Kevin Millhouse and too ashamed to let anyone know what had happened, except the two she made promise to never tell.

"Aww shoot, Tee," Sincere said, jumping up grabbing her phone from the night stand, dialing her favorite cousin's number.

"Hello," Tyra answered.

"Why aren't you still at school lil girl?" Sincere asked, surprised that she answered.

"Why are you calling me during my school hours?" Tyra replied, laughing. Sin asked, "What's up cuz?"

"First who's around you?" Sincere asked, cautiously.

"Girl no one, I'm in my room, you must got some tea? If you do, give it to me and don't leave out the sugar," Tyra replied, with her ears glued to her phone." "Well, things been crazy here in the "A" this last week girl." Sincere took a deep breath and said, "Tee I'm pregnant."

It was complete silence on the other end of the phone. Sincere asked "Tee are you there?"

"Yeah, I'm here cuz. You just shocked me with this news. You're telling me Kevin got you pregnant that night in August, Sin? That Bastard! What are you going to do?" Tyra asked, concerned.

"Well Tee, I have an appointment, November 4th to end the pregnancy, after that, I just want to forget this ever happened."

The girls talked a little longer, and then they hung up; Sincere fell asleep.

Chapter 6

NOVEMBER 4TH

Sincere stared at the clock. It was 6am and time was ticking away. Today's the day she'd been waiting to come; November 4th, the day she would end her pregnancy.

"*Knock knock*," Neicy said, knocking on her daughter's door before entering.

"Morning momma, what time is it?" I must have dozed back off," Sincere said, rubbing her eyes, stretching, looking at her very pregnant mother.

"It's eight thirty, baby girl," she answered, rubbing her belly.

"Eight thirty, shoot, I got to get up."

Sincere jumped up and headed to her bathroom.

"Baby girl, do you have plans this morning?" Her mother asked, still rubbing her belly, taking a bite of a glazed donut and walking towards Sincere's bathroom door.

"No, not really, me and Shay were gonna do some early morning shopping, then maybe catch a movie or have lunch," Sincere answered, washing her face.

"Aww, baby girl, I was hoping you'd come to the doctor with me today, I find out what this bun in my oven is. I'm asking because your father had an important meeting this morning and can't come along, so who's next in line to take his place? Our lil sunshine," Neicy smiled, waiting for Sincere to answer.

She glanced up at her mother, who looked excited about her going to this doctor's appointment with her.

"Oh, alright, I'll go momma; let me get dressed and I'll be down in a second."

“Great, I'll be waiting downstairs for you.” Neicy waddled out of Sincere's room and down the hall.

Sincere hurried to her phone, dialing Shay’s number. Shay picks up, “Hello.”

“Shay it's me, Sin. Change of plans for this morning girly. My mom wants me to go with her to the doctor at 9:45am. She finds out what she's having today.”

“Damn Sin. what are you going to do about your own appointment today at ten o clock? ” Shay asked.

“That's why I'm calling you, I need you to call the clinic for me and make a new appointment for next Saturday same time. Hurry call now and call me right back.”

Sincere hung up the phone, waiting for Shay to call back.

“*RING*,” Sincere picked up the phone on the first ring, Hello…Shay?” Yeah Sin, it’s me, and I don’t have good news.” She sounded disappointed. “What?” Sincere was nervous and her heart beat fast.

“You have to go this Tuesday at 10am or you'll be waiting another two to three weeks and you don't have time to wait. You have to get rid of that Millhouse that's growing inside of you. Sin you are starting to show,” Shay said, determined.

Sincere slumped down on her bed.

“Well Tuesday at ten it is; we'll just have to miss school. Thanks Shay, but I gotta go, my momma's waiting for me. I'll call you later,” Sincere said.

“Sincere are you almost ready?” Neicy yelled up the stairs.”

Yes momma, I'm coming.”

Sincere rushed down the stairs where her mother awaited.

"Oh good baby girl, you're ready. If I put one more thing in my mouth, I'm going to gain another hundred pounds before I reach the doctor's office," Neicy laughed, walking out the door.

They had a long wait. The doctor was running behind.

"Neicy Simmons," the nurse hollered, flinging the door open.

"Finally," Sincere thought, as her and her mother walked back to the room for the ultrasound. "It's a girl," the doctor said, pointing to the small screen, where they could see a tiny little life moving.

"Aww, a sister momma, I'll have a little sister, I couldn't be happier." Sincere rubbed her mother's hand.

"Me either, baby girl; two little sunshine's for me and your father. I think he wants a boy though. They both smiled.

It was Tuesday, November 7th and Sincere was awakened by her phone ringing, loudly, "Hello," she answered.

"Sin it's me, Shay. Wake up girl; we have a long day ahead of us. So get up, act like it's a normal school day, and I'll be at your house by seven thirty, alright."

"Alright," Sincere hung up the phone and prepared for her day. On this day, her nightmare pregnancy would finally be over.

At the clinic it seemed like Sincere and Shay had been waiting an eternity for their number to be called.

Then they heard the nurse call, "S.S.S-34," because on this side of the clinic, no names were used, only initials and a number.

As she entered the double doors, Sincere's heart beat faster than it ever had before.

Hi honey, my name is Michelle and I'm going to be

the nurse in here with you the whole time. You can hold my hand or squeeze it if you have to, OK?" The nurse smiled and asked Sincere to remove her clothes and she and the doctor would return in a few minutes.

Sincere gave half a smile and nodded. As she undressed, her heart beat rapidly, her hands shook, and her skin was slippery with sweat.

"Oh Lord, be with me," she said, as she lay back waiting for Nurse Michelle and the doctor to return.

She heard a knock at the door. A tall skinny woman walked in with long black wavy hair and bright eyes.

"Hello Sincere, I'm Dr. Richardson. I'll be doing your procedure this morning. At any time if you need me to stop for a minute, let me know," Dr. Richardson said, smiling.

"Okay," Sincere said, lying back apprehensively.

"Okay honey, first I'm going to numb you. I have to stick you three times," Dr. Richardson said, pulling out a needle that looked to be a foot long.

"Okay Sincere sweetheart, you're going to feel a lot of pressure, some pulling, and tugging. I need you to either close your eyes or look up at the wall and hold my nurses hand," she said, turning on a machine, getting ready to perform Sincere's procedure.

"Oh God, ouch, oh my God, it hurts, I feel you pulling. Ouch! Please hurry, please hurry… It hurts so bad." Sincere screamed, almost breaking the nurse's hand while trying to look up at the wall.

"Oh God, I can't take it anymore, are you done?" Sincere asked, while turning her head to the

right, something she wished she had never done. Sincere saw her unborn child being sucked out through a tube and into a black garbage bag, in a small grey container.

Tears began to flow from Sin's eyes. *How could I do this to my innocent unborn baby, she thought to herself?*

The machine was turned off and the procedure ended.

“Okay Sincere, I'm going to help you to the restroom and to get dressed. You might feel some cramping and you may also have some clotting. Just let me know, I'm here for you,” Nurse Michelle grabbed Sincere's hand, helping her to the restroom.

Sincere comes out the restroom and Nurse Michelle is waiting for her to guide her into another room. This room had four other girls in there resting, eating cookies, and drinking orange juice. “Would you like something to drink and some cookies honey?” They will help your blood get back pumping.”

Nurse Michelle hands Sincere four cookies and a cup of cold orange juice.

“Can my best friend comeback here? Sincere asked while biting one of the cookies.

”Of course,” I'll go get her for you, sweetie,” Nurse Michelle said, while, leaving the room with a smile and returns with Shay.”

Hey Sin how you feeling?” Shay said, as she walks in giving her best friend a hug.

”I'll be fine, just need some rest. I feel so weak right now,” Sincere said, as she sips her orange juice.

They are in the recovery room for about an hour when Nurse Michelle comes back and said,” Sincere you can leave now honey, remember get some rest. No lifting, get some pain medicine if you it and make a follow up appointment in two weeks.”

Leaving the clinic Shay helps a weak Sincere get into the car and drives her best friend home. On the way to Sin's house it was so quiet you could hear a pin drop on the car floor. Neither one of the girls said, anything.

”We're here bestie. Do you need me to come in with you? Shay said, as she pulls as close to Sincere's front door as possible.

"Naw, I'll be ok. I'm gonna take a shower and climb into bed. I'll give you a call in a few hours," Sincere said, as she opened the car door and walks to her front door.

She started walking up the stairs and stills feels very weak from what she just endured. So the walk up the stairs she had taken many times before seemed as if it was taking a lifetime. Finally reaching her bedroom, Sincere took a hot shower, got into her soft king size canopy bed, and goes to sleep. She just wants to forget this day ever happened!

Chapter 7

THE NEW ADDITION

It was a windy but warm March night in Atlanta and everyone in the Simmons mansion was sound asleep.

Momma! Momma! Sincere heard a small voice crying, it was coming from her bathroom. So she sat up on her bed to listen to see if she'll hear it again. And she did!

Momma; this time Sincere hopped off her bed and walks towards her bathroom. She gently opened the door barely peeking in, “Damn I can't see anything,” she said, to herself.

She opened her bathroom door a little more so she could see where this strange noise was coming from; she see's blood and tiny footprints tracking through the blood. Her eyes get BIG with fear as she continues to walk further into her bathroom.

OOOOOOOOOOOOAH, she screamed as she looked at a baby boy with the cord still attached to him. The baby was cut up in a black garbage bag with his bloody face hanging out crying out, Momma...."NOOOO!"

Sincere jumps up in a cold sweat, “Whew it was just another bad dream,” she took a deep breath and goes to throw some cold water on her face to wake completely up, because she don't feel like sleeping.

Sincere decides she'll go to the kitchen to have a glass of warm milk, as she reaches the kitchen she sees her mother walking around taking deep breaths.

“Momma are you having contractions? Why didn't you wake someone?” Sincere started to rub her mother's back looking concerned.

“O baby girl this had only been going on thirty minutes now, I'll wait another hour to see how strong they come, I don't want to rush to the hospital right away, she said, still taking deep breaths.

“Well I'm going to time your contractions,” Sincere said, as she got the watch out of the kitchen drawer.

"Momma, are you having another contraction? If you have two more within the next ten minutes, I'm waking daddy!”

Okay baby, I won't argue with you,” Neicy said, in pain blowing now instead of taking deep breaths.

A few minutes go by and Sincere hears WATER DRIPPING ONTO THE FLOOR.

"Oh shit my water just broke baby girl, go wake your father, tell him to grab my bag I'm going to call Dr. Sharp and let him know it's time. “Neicy said, nervously to Mimi and Sincere. Excited but nervous at the same time for her mother, Sincere ran to wake her father who was sound asleep. She then got dressed herself to watch the birth of her new baby sister.

At the hospital Sincere and her father both await the arrival of the new baby girl and watched as Neicy in pain struggle through her contractions.

“O God, I have to push,” Neicy yelled to a nurse who just walked in.

“NO WAIT DON'T PUSH let me get the doctor in here,” the nurse said, running out to the hall.

"HURRY,” Sammy said, concerned for his wife who's ready to give birth.

"*PUSH* Baby *PUSH*.” “Yeah momma *PUSH*.” Sincere and Sammy are coaching Neicy to push their new addition into the world.

A soft cry is heard throughout the small labor room. Neicy gave birth to a 7pound 4oz twenty inch beautiful baby girl.

"She's beautiful momma," Sincere hugs her mother to congratulate her on a good job delivering her new little sister.

"She's a beautiful baby, looking just like my dad" Sammy said, taking pictures with tears of joy rolling down his cheeks."

Ahh, she does look like your father honey, "Let's name her Samantha Joy Simmons," Neicy said, very exhausted."

Samantha Joy Simmons, I like it," Sammy said, smiling, taking a picture of his three favorite girls.

"Yeah, I like it too momma. We will call her Sami as a nickname," Sincere gave her mom a smile.

"SAMANTHA JOY SIMMONS welcome to the world, now our family is complete," Neicy said, as she looked at her family and smiled.

"Yeah baby our family is now complete," Sammy smiled and the Simmons family enjoyed the day with their new addition!

Chapter 8

BIG EIGHTEEN

Happy Birthday Sunshine. Sincere's parents and Mimi yelled loudly as they burst into sleeping Sincere's bedroom with balloons and breakfast with a candle in the blueberry muffin.

"Awww," Sincere said, pulling her covers over her head. THANK YOU. But can I brush my teeth first before I start giving out kisses for my birthday wishes and breakfast?

Sincere got out of bed, took a shower, and threw on her favorite Donna Karan sundress and sandals before she headed downstairs, where her parents were waiting.

"HURRY, HURRY," Sammy said, rushing his eighteen year old daughter downstairs.

"I'm comin', I'm comin'," Sincere said, running down the stairs almost out of breath.

"Open the door and look outside," Neicy said, while holding 4 four month old Samantha. Sincere opened the front door to see a Silver 1993 drop top Mercedes Benz with a big pink bow around it, screaming loudly.

"Momma, daddy, THANK YOU; THANK YOU SO MUCH!" Sincere said, hugging her parents so tight with her leg halfway in the driver's seat of her brand new car.

"Can I take it for a spin?" she said, looking at her parents with those pretty green eyes they can never say no to.

"Of course, it's yours," Sammy answered.

"BEEP! BEEP! BEEP!" Sincere blew her horn while sitting outside her best friend Shay's mansion.

"Who the hell honking like that? We don't live

outside, this not Orchard Ct projects," Shay yelled out her bedroom window.

"Then why are you yelling out a window like we're in the projects girl?" Sincere said, out her car window to Shay.

"Aye, is this your new ride?" Shay said, running to open the passenger side door of the drop top Benz her best friend now owned.

"Yep she's all mine, my parents got it for my eighteenth birthday, I named her Angel," Sincere said, rubbing her steering wheel.

"Oh shoot, with all the excitement about the car I almost forgot, happy eighteenth birthday bitch, I love you!" Shay said, to Sincere hugging her.

"Now let's take Angel for a ride," Shay looked at Sin clicking her seatbelt giving her the hint to start rolling the car out her driveway.

"It's going down already in downtown ATL and it's only 12 p.m. , tonight's going to be banana's, "Shay said, overly excited, turning up the music popping her fingers as they cruised down Peachtree St.

"Yep perfect for my birthday weekend. Me, U, and Angel will be hitting the ATL nightlife tonight, I'm ready to be seen. "The A needs to know who Sincere Sunshine Simmons is". Sincere said, as she looked in her rearview mirror and licks her lips.

The girls are cruising downtown Atlanta loving everything they see and they can't wait for the sun to go down and the moon to come out.

"I'm coming to your crib for a lil bit, "Shay said to Sin as she glosses her lips.

"Cool we can chill till we figure out what we doing tonight. I'm eighteen and legal and we are going to get into something for sure. We live in Hotlanta, one of the hottest spots around," Sincere said, as she got on the highway to head home.

As Sincere turned down her street, Shay looked over and said,

"Hey Sin you need to park in y'all six car garage, you have a spot in it now, let's say we take the back way so you can park Angel in the garage."

"You're right; I do have a spot in the garage now. I'm taking the back road and parking Angel in daddy's garage," Sincere said, turning the car around to take the back road to their garage to park her brand new 1993 Drop top Benz in it.

As they pull into the garage, Sincere had the biggest grin on her face. The feeling was priceless, having her own car to park in the garage every day. The young ladies grab their bags and head into the house.

Surprise! Everyone yelled throwing confetti with big smiles on their faces.

"Oh My God," Sincere said, looking happy, surprised and scared all at the same time.

"I had no idea! This is such a surprise! I love all of you!"

Tears of joy rolled down Sincere's face as she kisses her aunts, uncles, cousins, parents and other guests that had shown up to celebrate her eighteenth birthday.

"Yeah bestie, I knew the whole time, it took everything in me not to tell you, because you know I can't hold water when it comes to giving you the 411. I did it though, plus kept you gone four hours so your parents could set up everything. I'm exhausted, "Shay gave Sincere a big hug and they laughed.

Sincere walked around the mansion realizing how many family and friends were there to help celebrate her birthday.

She said, to the mansion full of guests, "Wow, I'm so happy all of you came to be with me on my eighteenth birthday you have made this day even more special for me. I thank you all for coming."

"Happy birthday Sin, did you miss me, cousin?"

Sincere turns around, and then all you hear was a loud scream throughout the mansion.

"Tyra, you're here! I thought you guys didn't make it."

Sincere and Tyra hug for what seems like an hour before she gave her Uncle Steve a big hug and thanked him for making her party. Sammy and Neicy had done it extremely big for their oldest daughter's eighteenth birthday. All of Buckhead was there. This would be a night for Sincere to remember.

Sincere started mingling, enjoying the party, and all the people there were laughing, when Tyra, Shay, and Sincere glanced over by the tennis court where she saw Keke, Keithen, Tavarious, Skeeter. Further off to the side she saw Kevin Millhouse. Sincere felt fire run through her body, her heart started beating fast with rage.

"How dare this son of a bitch show up to my party at my home," Sincere thought to herself as she started walking towards the tennis court where the young men were standing.

"Hey guys what's up? Thanks for coming to my party. Why don't you guys go fix yourselves a plate, it's plenty of good food up there."

"Food, yes sir, don't have to ask me twice" Keke said, rubbing his hands together, giving the guys the hint to follow him to the food.

As they walked off, Sincere grabbed Kevin's arm and said, "Hey Kevin not you, let me talk to you in private for a minute."

Sincere let Keke and the other guys get further away, and then asked Kevin to follow her.

Before she can get to the Gazebo, she lashed out at Kevin and said, "What the hell are you doing here, are you crazy, showing up to my party like you didn't rape me?

"Sincere, I apologize for hurting you; I don't know

what came over me that night. I had been drinking; you were looking so good to me. I wanted you so bad I just lost all control of myself. Please forgive me, I never meant for that to happen, not that way anyhow," Kevin tried to grab Sincere's hand hoping she'd find it in her heart to forgive him for the terrible thing he did that August night in 1992.

"No Kevin, I will not hold your hand and I will not accept your apology. However, I will give you five minutes to speak your peace before I show you the way out," Sincere gave Kevin an evil look as she waited to see what else he had to say.

"Look Sincere for whatever it's worth, I'm sorry. What happened that night never should have happened, I apologize deeply again. I hope you will forgive me one day, so I can put this behind me, and never bother you again," Kevin looked down at the ground while waiting for Sincere to respond.

"Umm, tell me exactly what are you apologizing for Kevin? Are you apologizing for raping me and taking my virginity against my will? Or are you apologizing for getting me pregnant, leaving me to sneak to get an abortion? Or are you apologizing for the nightmares I have every night since the abortion? Tell me Kevin, what the hell exactly are you apologizing for?" Sincere said, slapping Kevin as hard as she could.

Before Kevin could get anything else out his mouth Sincere yelled, "Get the hell off my property and don't ever return here again, Kevin. If you ever come near me again, I'll make you sorry you did! Do you hear me Kevin; I'll make you sorry if you come near me again! Now leave before this birthday celebration turns very ugly."

Kevin started to open his mouth to say one last thing to Sincere, and then decided not to. He shook his head and walked off leaving the Simmons mansion.

Sincere joined her family and friends to finish

celebrating her day which everyone enjoyed. This was another priceless Simmons family moment.

Chapter 9

LEX

The phone rings, loudly, waking the young ladies up!

"Ugh, get that for me," Sincere, Tyra asked.

"Hey Sincere?" A deep sexy voice said, on the other end of the line.

"No this is her cousin Tee, Who's this?" Tyra asked.

The deep voice answered, "This is Lex, I met Sincere downtown yesterday, is she in?"

Lex's voice sounded real good to Tyra, so she shook Sincere saying, "Girl wake up, it's a guy on the phone named Lex and he sounds real nice looking," Tyra smiled, putting the phone to Sincere's ear, who was still half asleep.

"Hello," Sincere said, lifting herself off of her pillow. "Hello sexy, I was calling to see do you had any plans for later today?" Lex waited for Sincere to answer him.

"Well no, not really. My cousin is here from Cali, so we'll get into something, I'm sure," Sincere said, giving Tyra and Shay the thumbs up.

Lex said, "I'm having a pool party at my place, it starts at 7pm, you and your friends are welcome to come. Your presence would be appreciated. Hope to see you there." "Seven pm, OK, cool; give me your address and we'll swing through."

Sincere snapped her fingers for Tyra to hand her the pad of paper and pen to take down his address and then hangs up the phone. Sincere hopped off the bed and did her booty dance, while singing.

"We're going to a pool party in Roger Lake Estates tonight."

"You know I'm down for whatever, Shay said, brushing her teeth."

"I'm down too, but first tell me about this Lex," Tyra said, putting more toothpaste on her toothbrush.

"We met Lex yesterday; his real name is Alex Foster. He's 22yrs old, 6'5, short wavy hair, nice dark coffee brown skin, perfect white teeth with big brown eyes, that'll make you melt and he has his own business."

Sincere was all smiles as she continued talk about Lex to her cousin.

It was after 7pm and Sincere was rushing her cousin and friend to get dressed so they could get to the pool party that sexy ass Lex was having at his house.

"Can you two slow pokes put a move on it, the party started at 7:00 PM? I want to get there. I'm sure Lex is waiting for me, to make my entrance." Sincere said, rubbing her hands down the side of her Sexy black Versace strapless dress.

"I'm ready," Tyra walked out of the bathroom fixing her sexy red Nicole Miller dress. "We're waiting on Ms. Shay to get finished."

Shay walked out in a long white Christian Dior dress saying, "No, sweet pea's Ms. Shay is ready, willing and able, let's go"!

They pull up to Roger Lake Estates. The ladies were impressed by what they saw.

"Hmm, Mr. Alex Foster has a little paper, huh Sincere?" Shay chuckled.

"I have no idea girly, but I guess we're about to find out. Let's make our entrance so we can have all eyes on us."

Sincere dropped her drop top and they proceeded to walk to Lex's front door. They saw a sign that read, *Pool party this way*. The girls headed to the back, where they saw sexy men everywhere and half naked females running around in swim suits."

“Hey you came,” Lex said, as he approached Sincere and the other ladies.

“I told you we would be here, so here we are.” Sincere gave Lex a smile with her eyes.

“Glad you could make it, Sincere, wow you’re a sight for sore eyes, you look real good tonight.” Lex reached out to give Sincere a hug, and then said, “OH my God, you smell good enough to eat, where have you been all my life?”

“I don't know where I've been all your life, but the important thing is I'm in your life now. Good things come to those who wait.” Sincere rubbed Lex’s face and then blew him a kiss.

“Ooh, Sincere you don't know what you just did to me girl,” pulling Sincere closer to him, asking her and her friends to come meet some of his friends.

They walk into Lex’s kitchen where it was four men standing around joking. Lex introduces Sincere, Shay and Tyra to his friends. I told ya’ll about Sincere and these beautiful ladies are her cousins, Tyra and her best friend, Shay. Ladies this is my brother, Antonio, my cousins Brian and Paul and this big guy here is my right hand man, Aaron.”

Everyone shared words and then Lex asked,” do either of you ladies want something to drink or eat, there's plenty to go around?”

“Something to drink would be nice, what do you have?” Sincere asked Lex, giving him eye contact with her almond shaped green eyes.”

“Whatever you want, nine times out of ten I have it. If I don't, we can go get it,” giving Sincere the same look back while licking his lips, gently.

“Well do you have *Alize* with a hint of OJ?” Sincere asked.

Why I sure do have that for you sexy lady,” Lex grabbed a few glasses and made three drinks for the ladies.

They sipped their drinks while enjoying each other's company. Sincere got an uncomfortable feeling, reminding her of how she got raped in August of 1992. She watched everyone carefully, especially the four men, Lex had introduced them to earlier. She looked at Lex's brother Tonio first. Tonio was 6ft, he was much darker than Lex and his front tooth was chipped, but he was a cutie, Sincere thought. She took a look at the cousins, Brian and Paul who were twins, and were double the pleasure. These men were 6'6, light smooth skin with dark facial features, chestnut brown eyes, body's with tattoo's covering their arm's and chest.

Brian had waves in his hair and a mustache. His twin Paul was bald with a beard nicely groomed. Sincere thought both men were equally sexy and laid back. Then Sincere took a look at Aaron, who was 5'9, and as black as Sincere's dress, with cold dark brown eyes. His smile was nice, which added to his charm. However, it was something in Aaron's eyes that made her skin crawl. She thought to herself, “Shit, I better watch this Aaron, something's not right about him.”

“Oh wow, it's 2am already,” Tyra said, looking at her Tissot watch. ”I hate to be the party pooper guys, but Sin we have to be leaving soon, my plane leaves at 10am.”

“Yeah, she's right Lex, I do have to get her to the airport early, so we better wrap this up, however, it's been really nice kicking it with y'all. “Thanks again for the invitation Lex,” Sincere said, gathering their things to leave Lex's house.

When they got in the car, Shay said, “Ok did y'all peep how fine that Paul was, I gots to have him. I have plans for him and they aren't dinner plans either,” the girls laugh.

“I think his brother Brian was pretty hot, but I don't know, Tonio sexy too,” Tyra said, poking her lips out, as if she couldn't decide which one of the men she liked the most.

“But did y'all peep how weird Lex's friend Aaron

looked. Well, let me not say weird but scary. I got an evil vibe from him."

Sincere looked over in the passenger seat at Tyra, waiting for either of the girls to respond. "Yeah, he seems cool, but his eyes tell a different story." Tyra said, agreeing with her cousin. "Well I'm going to be real bitches; I didn't notice anyone but Paul." Shay said, laughing, but very serious about what she had just said.

They got to Sincere's house and they all instantly prepared to sleep a few hours before taking

Tyra to the airport.

Ring, ring... the phone rang.

Sincere thought who the hell is calling me this late?

She picks up, "Hello."

"Hey sexy, I know it's late, but I had to make sure you made it home safely and I wanted to ask you how about breakfast after you take your cousin to the airport in a few hours, we could talk and get to know each other better?"

"Okay Lex, I'd like that, I'll give you a call in the morning before we head out." Sincere hung up the phone and drifts off to sleep fast.

The alarm sounded at 7:30 am; the girls jumped up, rushing to get things together, to get Tyra to the airport.

When they got in the car, Shay said, "Hey, girly, drop me off at home; I'm tired to even ride, plus you got a breakfast date with Lex. By the way, while you're having breakfast chatter, find a way to mention me, and make it so me and Paul can meet again, Ya feel me Sin?"

Sincere shook her head, giving a slight grin, saying, "Yeah bestie, I feel ya."

Sincere and Tyra finally pulled up to the airport. Sin helped Tyra with her bags. They gave each other the usual hugs and kisses before they both shed a few tears.

"Call me once you get home Tee and don't forget either. I love you, have a safe flight."

Sincere turned to get in her car so she could meet Lex at one of the best Soul Food Restaurants in Atlanta, *U'Neek's Soul Food & Breakfast.*

Sincere pulled up in the parking lot. She saw Lex was just pulling up himself. She looked in her rearview mirror to freshen her lip gloss, making sure she looked okay before greeting him. When she got out of the car, she saw him approaching her with 18 pink roses.

"These are for you, I believe you said pink was your favorite color, correct?"

Lex hands Sincere the roses and she's gives him a kiss on the cheek and a smile. Over breakfast Sincere and Lex talk about everything. Before they knew it, they had been at the restaurant for over two hours.

"I could sit and talk to you forever Lex, but if I don't get any sleep I'm gonna collapse," Sincere laughs and rubs Lex's hand across the table.

"Alright, I'll let you end this breakfast date if you'll have dinner with me tonight," he said, looking into Sincere's green eyes while kissing her hand.

The kiss felt so good. Lex's lips were very soft and Sincere liked the way that felt, so she said, "Yes," to Lex's dinner proposal. They left U'Neek's to go their separate ways, until dinner tonight.

Sincere looked through her walk-in closet, trying to find the perfect outfit or dress to wear tonight. She wanted Lex's eyes to pop out of his head when he sees her for dinner. She picked up her phone and called Lex to let him know she'll be leaving her home in the next fifteen minutes.

Sincere drove to meet Lex at Maxwell's, one of the finest restaurants in downtown Atlanta. She couldn't help but smile; she was really feeling Lex and it's only been a few days. Sincere thought she'd never trust another man after what Kevin Millhouse had done. She had kept herself far away from men this year, fearing that she would let one get too close and he would do what Kevin had done. But it was something about Lex and Sincere wanted to know what that something was.

Sincere pulled up to MAXWELL'S, and the valet service guy gave her a ticket. She walked down the red carpet entering the double doors of this very elegant restaurant. As she walks in, there stood a handsome man holdings a pen and a list of names, saying, "Hi, welcome to Maxwell's, do you have reservations?"

"Why yes I have a dinner reservation with Alex Foster."

When he opened his mouth he caught Sincere by surprise, she couldn't figure out why such a handsome guy was gay. His voice and hand motions gave him away. Sincere has nothing against people who like the same sex, if they liked it, she loved it. She just didn't understand why a lot of the fine men in ATL were gay, but in a big city, anything can happen and anything goes. The host replied back to Sincere, "Oh you're a guest of Mr. Foster, come right this way, we'll have someone show you to his table."

As this short heavyset woman showed Sincere to Lex's table, she's thought, "Lex must come here often, and she wondered… hmm, which number am I? It seemed like Mr. Foster is known at Maxwell's. Now Sincere wanted to put her guard up, not because she thought he would rape her, but because she thought he was the playboy type and her daddy taught her better than to be some man's #2 or his plaything.

When she reached the table, Lex was there looking through the menu. He looked up and saw Sincere. He got up from his seat, kissed her, smiling and said, "Man, baby you look more amazing every time I see you, how do you do it?"

Sincere with her straight and pinned up, non-curly

hair-do, wearing a money green Chanel dress with matching money green accessories and snake skin Chanel heel's, which Sincere never wears, but Maxwell's was a classy place where Atlanta's most elite dine. So, she had to come with it...Sincere with her lips turned up, her eyebrow lifted responding to Lex's compliment, "I don't know how I do it Alex, but how many women have you ran that line on; I'm young but not stupid?"

"Wait, you called me Alex and the look on your face tells me you're serious not joking." Baby look I'm young myself, but I'm not trying to run game on you Sincere, I'm trying to get to know you to see where this can lead."

Lex grabbed Sincere's hands across the table, looking into her green eyes, hoping she could see the sincerity in what he just said.

Sincere took a deep breath and asked him, "Then why do the workers here know you so well, like you're always here, and I assume you're here with other women. So what Lex, is this the place you bring young ladies like myself to impress them, hoping to get in their pants after you've spent hundreds on a meal?"

Lex looked at Sincere sort of surprised by her thoughts. He couldn't help but to laugh at her assumption.

Sincere saw that what she said had Lex laughing and asked, "Did I say something funny Alex?"

Still laughing, Lex answered, "No baby, what you said wasn't funny, what you assumed was funny, because it's no truth to it. Sincere, I come here often with my father and other business partners for meetings. Remember I told you I had my own business?

Sincere nodded her head, indicating to Lex, that she was listening.

Lex continued to explain, "Well Sincere baby, it's not my own business, it's more like a company or corporation and I'm Vice President of Momma Foster's Cookies & Desserts. My father is the CEO of it. He named it Momma Foster's after my Nana who used to bake all the cookies and other delicious desserts herself before dying two years ago, now we just use her recipes."

Sincere looked surprised about who Lex was, but she felt so dumb inside for accusing him of trying to impress her to get in her pants. She rubbed Lex's hands, saying, "Lex, I'm so sorry for flying off the handle. It's just most men just want to get in a young girls pants and I don't want that. I've always said I wanted to save myself for my husband.

Sincere gave a smile and replied, "I have enjoyed this evening as well, Lex. It has been really nice getting to know you, and yes this is the first dinner of many more to come."

Driving home, all Sincere could think about was Lex. She couldn't wait to get home to call Shay and Tee and give them the tea. Pulling into the garage, she noticed her parents had just gotten in themselves, which was unusual, because her mother never liked to keep Baby Sami out late.

"That was an awfully long dinner sweetheart," Neicy said to Sincere, taking Baby Sami out of her carrier.

"Yeah, we stayed at Maxwell's until it closed. It was nice, I think I like him momma."

Sincere smiled, giving her baby sister a kiss. She noticed the baby felt warm, telling her mother,

"Hey, Sami is a little warm momma."

"Oh I know sweetheart, she has an ear infection. Your father and I are just getting in from the ER. It's going to be a long night for your father, he's not going into his office and I have a meeting with a client first thing, so I will not be up too much longer with my little angel."

Sincere laughs, saying, "Well good luck trying to have daddy stay up, he's already sleep."

Sincere pointed to the family room where her father was fast asleep, snoring in his favorite chair.

"Oh no, Sammy is not going to leave me up, I'm going to wake him by putting his precious pumpkin on his chest," Neicy headed towards the family room.

"Mom wait," Sincere yelled to stop her.

She got her mother's attention and said, "No daddy needs his rest too. Give me Sami. I'll take her in my room with me for the night, and I'll keep an eye on her while you're working tomorrow. Now give me the little crumb snatcher and get some rest, you have a long day tomorrow".

Neicy gave Sincere her baby sister, kissing both girls and then went to bed.

When she got to her room, Sincere made sure she got little Sami settled and asleep before she picked up the phone to call Shay and Tee.

Once she got her baby sister content, Sincere picked up her phone to call her favorite cousin, Tee.

"Hello," Tee answered, out of breath, "Ummm, why are you breathing so hard?" Sincere asked with a puzzled look on her face.

Tyra laughed and answered, "Get your mind out the gutter; I was exercising Sin."

Sincere laughed back and replied, "Well, let me know, answering the phone breathing heavy in the night hours doesn't sound good."

The young ladies laughed a bit then Sincere said, "Tee enough of this small talk, let's get to why I called you, but first let me click over to call Shay on three-way."

Sincere clicked over before she heard Tee say, "Wait heffa, why I can't hear first, why I gotta wait?"

Sincere rolled her eyes in her head and answered, "Tee cut it out because I don't want to repeat this twice. I want us all to be on the phone together, that way I can hear both of your opinions at one time. Now hold on, let me get Shay on the line."

"Yeah speak to me," Shay answered. "Oh my Shay, you're killing me with this new way of answering the phone. But anyway, listen up I got Tee on the line and I have some tea to share with you guys and it's heavy on the sugar with a lil bit of honey added."

Sincere told her cousin and best friend about her whole day with Alex Foster, aka Lex; from breakfast at U'Neek's to dinner at Maxwell's.

"Ooo, girl it sounds like Lex is really digging you; that's good. Now I can make my way in with Paul's fine ass," Shay made the conversation about her meeting Paul instead of Sincere giving them the tea on her and Lex.

After talking an hour, Sincere decided to let her girls off the phone so she could get some rest before her sick cranky little sister woke up for a diaper change or just some TLC, because she was ill.

"Hey ladies it's been real, but I have Sami in the room with me for the night, she's not feeling well, so I better get off the phone and try to get forty winks before she gets up." Sincere and the ladies said their goodbyes and then hung up. Just when she put on her pajamas, the phone rang.

She hurried to answer it before it woke her sleeping baby sister, "Hello," "Hey baby, it's me, Lex. I just had to tell you again I really enjoyed your company and I really like you Ms. Sincere Simmons."

Sincere was on the other end smiling. She too really liked Lex. They talked for thirty minutes before she told him she had to get some rest. Of course Lex, being the young gentleman he was, let Sincere off the phone and told her he'd call her sometime the next day. They hung up and Sincere finally got some rest.

It was January 2, 1994, the day after New Year's and

Lex's 23rd birthday. They had been officially dating for six months now, she thought. It was finally time to share something with him. Something she first thought she wouldn't share with any man until he put a ring on it. Yes, Sincere was ready to make love to him. She loved him, and the last six months of her life had been more than she could imagine; trips to Jamaica, Italy, and overnight flights to Vegas for fights. He bought her the most expensive things. Sincere was no stranger to high fashion, or money, but with Lex she felt something else along with that. Eighteen year old Sincere Simmons had fallen in love for the first time. Alex (Lex) Foster had stolen her heart and she loved him, and he would soon find out how much. Sincere was so excited as they p She knew tonight would be the night that she gave Lex, the man she loved, a part of herself that she'd never given any man, not willingly anyway. Lex opened the door and kissed Sincere. He told her to make herself at home. She kissed him back, and then told him she was going to use his restroom.

When Sincere got into the bathroom, she pulled out this very sexy purple teddy. She freshened up, puts the teddy on, and walked out the door. She stood in front of Lex, who was in his living room with R Kelly playing softly in the background. He had the fireplace going and was sitting on the couch with his eyes closed.

"I went through all of this and you sleep?" she said, kissing him so he'd open his eyes to see what he had standing in front of him.

"Wow! Sincere you look beautiful; you got this to wear for me?"

Lex stood up and kissed Sincere. She loved how his lips felt against her lips. They kissed for a little while longer, and then he took Sincere by her hand, laying her on his white mink rug in front of his fireplace. Sincere was nervous, as he gently took off her teddy, but she relaxed because that was what she wanted.

Once Lex had Sincere completely naked, he started rubbing her body, telling her how beautiful she was and how good she felt. Then he went down to her feet, rubbing them. As he rubbed, he placed her big toe in his mouth and began to lick, kiss and suck her body from her feet to the top of her head.

Lex kissed Sincere and said, “Do you like how you feel?”

Sincere’s body tingled, her vagina throbbing like it had a heartbeat, answering softly, “Yes, Lex, yes, I like it.”

Lex looked into Sincere’s green eyes, and said, “Well, let me know how you like this.”

He started kissing on her belly button and then he went further down to kiss the top of her vagina. He asked Sincere to open her legs a little bit for him, and she did.

When she opened her legs, Lex put his face down there.

Sincere stopped him and said,” Wait Lex, what are you doing?”

Lex answered, “I'm showing you, I love you and I want you to feel good. If you don't like it and want me to stop, just say the word and I'll stop, I promise, I won’t do nothing to hurt you.”

Sincere relaxes. When she does, Lex puts his face down there and starts to lick. Sincere had never felt anything like that in her life. The more he licked, the better it felt. The more wet she got; the more she moved her body in Lex’s face.

She began to moan loudly, “Ooo, Lex, don't stop, it feels so good! Please don't stop! I love it! I love it!”

When Lex heard Sincere say that, it made him start moving his tongue faster than the tornado that came and lifted Dorothy away to Oz! After Lex had been kissing

Sincere's body for thirty minutes, she began to shake uncontrollably, and could no longer take what he was doing, and pushed his head away saying, "No, No, I can't take no more, Stop!" Lex asked, "Are you sure?"

She said, no and pushed his face back down a little longer.

Sincere's body felt something so amazing, she thought she would explode. She moaned so loud, Lex neighbors probably heard her.

Lex looked up and asked Sincere again, "So how did you like that?"

She answered; I loved it and kissed Lex passionately. They made love all night and all day; they couldn't get enough of each other. There was no doubt in Sincere's mind, she had finally found her Mr. Right and she was going to be with him for as long as she could.

After thinking she would never trust a man again, she had found true love with Alex (Lex) Foster. She was happy, and the night she spent with him was the first night since Nov.7, 1992 that she didn't have a nightmare.

She had found her peace.

Chapter 10

LIFE WITH LEX

It's been two years since 21year old Sincere had grown into a 5'11, green eyed ravishing woman, who had committed herself to Alex (Lex) Foster. In those two years, she had grown a lot. She was no longer an 18year old young lady; she was a mature grown woman. She no longer wore her Louis Vuitton, DKNY, PRADA sandals; she upgraded to heels. She and Lex were happy and going strong.

He sold his house and bought a new home for him and Sincere to share together. He told her he saw a ring in the near future, and she was ecstatic about the idea of being Mrs. Alex Foster, Vice President of *Momma Foster's Cookies & Desserts.*

Sincere rushed home because tonight is Thursday, her night to make dinner for her and Lex. He loved her lasagna. So she planned to make lasagna, salad, garlic bread and she grabbed her favorite bottle of wine. She figured she'd be dessert.

Sincere lit the candles on the table when her sexy coffee brown man walked through the door. She let him know she was in the dining room.

"Baby I'm in here, dinner will be out on the table in a sec. I'm just lighting a few candles."

Lex walked in the dining room and saw Sincere in his favorite blue shirt with matching tie and some 6 inch ruby red heels. He licked his lips, asking her, "Baby can we skip dinner; I wanna go straight to dessert?"

Before Sincere could even answer, Lex had set her up on the dining room window sill, and began to make passionate love to her. Neither one of them ever thought twice about the open blinds, so every passing car could see Lex making love to Sincere.

For some reason being in the window turned Sincere on even more. She got down from the window, pushed Lex on a chair and kissed his sweet chocolate, {the kind not sold in stores} something she hadn't done their whole relationship. Lex couldn't believe what Sincere was doing.

In shock, but loving every moment of it, he grabbed her head pushing her further down on it. Telling her how much he loved her. They made love for the rest of the night.

“Guess I know what's for dinner tomorrow night,” Lex laughed, holding Sincere, as they drifted off to sleep in each other's arms.

Morning came and Sincere was in the kitchen cooking breakfast. When Lex came downstairs, he kissed her and mentioned a business plan that he, Aaron and Paul were thinking about looking into.

He sat at the table, eating his eggs and said, “So baby, the guys and I were thinking about opening a gentlemen's club in Roswell. I wanted to run this by you, because I want you to be a part of this. I want to share everything with you, you are my future wife.”

Sincere took a sip of her orange juice and replied, “A gentlemen's club,” “Lex that's a wonderful idea, but will it be stanking little hoochies running around everywhere, or will it be a classy establishment?”

Lex laughed. “Baby, have you ever known Alex Foster to do anything that wasn't classy and upscale, you don't have to ask me that; just let me know you’re in baby?” Sincere took a bite of her bacon and told him, “Yes,” asking for more details.

Lex said they wanted to call it, “*Peaches N Cream*”. They will have only the most beautiful women in Atlanta working there and it will be open 24 hours. The next few months Sincere helped Lex build his club that he's always dreamed of.

It was New Year's Day 1997, and the day before Lex's birthday. It was a big party going on at *Peaches N Cream* Gentlemen's Club. It had been a success, one of the hottest spots in Atlanta. The who's who of the businessmen, rap star's, NBA and NFL player's, and any man that had money had a membership with *Peaches N Cream*, where all of Hotlanta's finest worked.

So many came in to look at Georgia's *Peaches N Cream*, but left milked, because the women were so fine, all the men spent lots of cash. The party got too crowded for Sincere, so she headed toward the back to the office.

As she sat at the desk, looking in a mirror, wiping sweat from her forehead, a short Italian man with his shirt half opened wearing gold chains with greasy hair, and a small gut said, “Excuse me miss, are you the owner of this nice place?”

Sincere looked up from the mirror and said, “Why yes, I am co-owner, my name is Sincere Simmons. How may I help you Mr. “Reaching out to shake the man’s hand?

“Zanetti, Emanuel Zanetti of Zanetti Fashions in Italy,” the man said, in his Italian accent.

“Why it's nice to meet you Mr. Zanetti. Now again, how may I help you,” waiting for the man to answer?

Mr. Zanetti cleared his throat and asked Sincere if any of their girls escort gentlemen to events. He is in Atlanta often on business and would like a nice piece of eye candy on his arm to show off at his business meetings and dinners.

Sincere looked at him with a smile, asking him for his business card so she could arrange something, and get back with him some time tomorrow. Sincere went back to the party to finish celebrating the New Year with Lex on his birthday. It was a night to remember.

The next afternoon Sincere woke up, kissed Lex to wake him up, and let him know they were going to U'NEEK'S for a quick birthday lunch, and talk about a business proposition. They got dressed and had lunch. As they waited for their food, Sincere told Lex about Mr. Zanetti coming into the office last night and what he asked. She said Mr. Zanetti gave her a great idea. She could turn the empty building Lex owned next door, into *Peaches N Cream*, an escorting service slash massage parlor; that way men can see asses clap, enjoy good music and drink and if they like, come next door for a massage, a date or even a sexual fantasy (Not Sex). When Sincere said, sexual fantasy, she only meant setting up a few booths with phones so men could talk to a girl who would give him his fantasy. Sincere wanted to call it *House of Beauty* {Every man's fantasy}.

As Sincere finished telling Lex about her idea, she waited for him to respond.

Lex took a long drink of his ice tea and then told Sincere, “Baby, I think it's a go, I love your idea! We'll have a meeting with the girls to see which ones will be interested in doing this, and we'll go from there.

They finished their lunch and headed to *Peaches N Cream* to hold a meeting with the ladies. Out of the hundred ladies that were employed at the club, thirty of them were willing to go into business *House of Beauty* with Sincere. Sincere was very excited.

She lined it up so she could get Mr. Zanetti a date for the week he was in town and she could start working on floor plans for *House of Beauty*...It only took them two months to get up and running.

Sincere was so proud she had her own business and her father having nothing to do with it made her even more proud of her accomplishment. The money was coming in very fast from *Peaches N Cream* and *House of Beauty*.

Sincere and Lex both showered each other with gifts, loving their life together as a power couple. But what Sincere didn't know was Lex was planning on giving her a gift that would change their life together in a major way.

"I'll take it," Lex said, to the jeweler at Tiffany's, as he looked at a 5 carat diamond ring for his future wife.

Lex was happy about the decision he was about to make. Sincere had been the love of his life three years now, he couldn't live without her and he was finally going to show her she was all he ever wanted.

Lex called Sincere from his cell phone and told her he had a surprise for her and for her not to come home until 8pm. He should have everything set up by then. Sincere was a little puzzled but agreed to meet him at home by 8pm.

She hung up the phone and thought to herself "What does this man have up his sleeve?"

Many thoughts ran through Sincere's mind. She had been with Lex three years now and with him it could be anything. He could tell her at 8pm she has five minutes to pack because they're going to Paris. Her thoughts were endless. She smiled, while pulling into *Piedmont Women's Health Center.*

Sincere had a horrible memory of this clinic, but she was fond of the doctors and nurses there. It was their jobs to care for women in whatever way they were asked. She entered through the double doors; walked up to the desk where the receptionist was making copies of something, so she didn't see Sincere standing there.

Sincere cleared her throat to let the receptionist know she was there. The tall blonde, blue eyed woman said, in a heavy southern accent with a big smile. "Oh I'm sorry darling; I didn't see you standing there. How may I help you, do you have an appointment?"

Sincere gave a big smile back, "Yes, my name is

Sincere Simmons and I have a 3:15pm appointment with Dr. Washington."

The receptionist typed in her information, giving her papers to fill out telling her she'd be called shortly.

"Sincere Simmons" the nurse said, as she looked down at her clip board, opening the door.

Sincere stood up and followed the nurse in the room to have her yearly check-up with Dr. Washington. She finished her exam and got dressed to leave her appointment when there was a knock at the door.

"Come in" Sincere said.

It was Dr. Washington. She looked at Sincere's chart and said, "I had to catch you before you left. Some of the test results came back, so, I have some news to share with you if you would sit down for a moment."

Sincere became nervous, as she took a seat. Dr. Washington still hadn't said what the news was. She was thinking one of two things; she could be pregnant and Lex would be out of his mind with excitement, or she had some type of STD and she would have to kill Lex.

Sincere's heart pounded. She hesitated and then asked, "What's the news Dr. Washington.?" Dr. Washington sat down in the chair in front of Sincere and said, "Well Sincere honey, you are eight weeks pregnant. You and your boyfriend can expect your new son or daughter around October 14th. Congratulations!"

Sincere was overwhelmed by the news, but very happy she and Lex would be sharing something more than sex, dinner's, vacations and finances. They would be sharing a baby, a special part of them, made from love. This feeling was different from the first time Sincere had gotten pregnant; she was excited and couldn't wait to become a mother. In her heart, she knew Lex would be a great father. Sincere got in her white 97 Jaguar, a gift from Lex, only because he bought himself a black one and wanted Sincere's car and plates to match his. Their plates read C.E.O. 1 and C.E.O. 2. As she pulled out of the clinic, she dialed Lex from her cell phone and then paused, "No, I'll save this news for tonight," she thought to herself and then pushed the end button. She started to call her cousin Tee to tell her the good news.

"Hey Sin," Tyra answered.

"Hey Tee, cuz, I have some tea to spill to you." "Well, let me hear it girly and don't leave it out the sugar," Tyra said.

Sincere waited to tell her what she had to say. Sincere finally screamed with excitement, "I'm eight weeks pregnant."

"Ahh, Sin that's great news, when are you due?" "What did Lex say," asked Tyra?

Tyra started asking 99 questions. Sincere couldn't even answer one before Tyra was asking another one. She was so excited her cousin was having a baby by someone she loved this time.

Sincere laughed, as Tee threw all these questions at her, then said "Slow down Tee damn, let me answer your first two questions, then we'll go down your list."

"I'm due October 14th and Lex hasn't said anything because I haven't told him yet. I'm waiting til tonight.

He has something planned, so I'll just give him the news then."

"Well girl don't let him know you told me first because I'd never hear the end of it," Tyra laughed.

Sincere laughed back, "Oh don't worry, I won't mention I told you first. Neither one of us would hear the end of it, if I did." They talk a while longer, then Sincere let's Tee know she'll call her tomorrow to let her know how Lex reacted to the news.

She hung up with Tyra and dialed Shay's number to

see if she was home. She had to go somewhere to waste time. Lex didn't want her home until 8pm and it was only 5:30pm.

Shay answered, "What up Sinny Sin Sin Boo?"

Sincere pulled into a *Benny's Chicken N Biscuits,* because she was starving said, "Nothing, I was seeing if you were home. Lex has a surprise for me and don't want me home until 8pm, plus I have something juicy to tell you."

"Okay. I'm at the crib boo; they can you grab me some Tops," Shay asked.

"Tops, oh alright, I guess I can, I'm at Benny's getting us something to eat, I'll grab your *Tops* and I'll be there?"

Sincere hung up the phone, ordered their food, stopped to get Shay's *Tops* and then headed to Shay's downtown condo over-looking all of Atlanta.

Sincere had a key to Shay's place, so she could just walk right in. When she got in, Shay was sitting on the couch drinking some wine and puffing on a joint. "Hey do you wanna hit this," Shay said, handing the joint to Sincere expecting her to hit it.

"Naw, I'll pass on it for right now homie, well at least for the next seven months anyway."

Sincere looked at Shay smiling, hoping she comprehended what she said, even though she was high.

"The next seven months, why for the next seven months; Ahh, shit bitch, you pregnant? Ahh, hell yeah I'm going to be an Auntie."

Shay started dancing around her living room, grabbing Sincere's arms, trying to dance with her.

"Hey so what did the happy father to be say about this news. I know he's too happy about this," Shay asked, Sincere still dancing?

Sincere stopped dancing with Shay and took a few breaths and said, "Lex doesn't know yet, I'm waiting to tell him tonight, once I get home and hear what he has to tell me first.

I'm sure he'll be more excited than me and I probably won't be able to lift a finger if it's up to him." The girls eat their chicken and begin talking about how much Sincere and Lex's lives are about to change with this new bundle of joy coming in only seven short months.

In the middle of their conversation, Sincere's cell phone rings. It was Lex, calling to tell her he has everything set up and ready at home but he still wants her to wait until 8pm because he has to run to *Peaches N Cream* to handle some business with his right hand man, Aaron.

Sincere told Lex it was fine and that she was at Shay's passing time, and that she can't wait to see him. She told him she had something great to tell him. They hang up the phone and Sincere finished talking and watching TV with Shay to pass time until 8pm. That's when she would tell Lex he was going to be a father and would hear whatever it was he wanted to tell her.

Sincere was hoping it wasn't another vacation. She didn't want to take a vacation pregnant, and she wouldn't be able to enjoy it.

"Hmm, maybe he's going to pop the big question," she thought to herself, still watching TV with Shay, looking at the clock to see it was 7:25pm. As they watched their favorite show…***BREAKING NEWS*** flashed across the screen. The news reporter was in front of *Peaches N Cream* and said, "I'm at the scene of what looks like an attempted robbery gone bad, and I have heartbreaking news to deliver. Local businessman, ALEX FOSTER, has been shot and killed outside of his business this evening. Police are still investigating, if anyone knows or has seen anything; please contact the Roswell Police Department."

Sincere's mind went into a daze. She couldn't believe what she had just seen and heard. Lex was shot and killed. Her body shook terribly. All she could think of was who.

Who would want to hurt her Lex, a man that gave to everyone? Tears rolled down her face, and she started to feel sick to her stomach. She ran over to Shay's kitchen sink to vomit. She was devastated at what had happened to the love of her life. Everything they had planned to have together, any future they might have had has now been snatched from her, so unexpected and so sudden.

Sincere fell into Shays arms and cried more than she had ever cried before. What happened to Lex was killing her inside. They would never be married and what hurt her most, was the fact Lex will never know he was going to be a father.

Chapter 11

LIVING WITHOUT LEX

Sincere was still very shaken up and still crying a river in disbelief that someone had killed Lex. She couldn't bear the thought of going to the hospital to see Lex dead. She wanted to go home with thoughts that it was all a dream and her Lex would be walking in their door with his big smile so they could have their special night they planned together; but that would never happen now.

As they pulled up to Sincere and Lex's home, Sincere's body started to shake again. Her stomach cramped and tears flowed steadily, but she got the strength to get out of the car and walk into their home.

When Sincere and Shay walked into the house, it was like a scene from a movie. Lex had arranged pink rose petals and candles, leading from the doorway all the way to their bedroom, which the girls followed. On the bed, there were rose petals shaped into a heart; in the middle of the heart was Sincere's favorite chocolate candy. It spelled out, WILL YOU MARRY ME with a box from TIFFANY'S.

Sincere wiped the tears from her eyes and opened the box to see a 5 carat, diamond ring Lex had bought for her. In the box, was a note that said, "Sincere baby, I don't know what my life is going to bring in the future, all I know is my future won't be worth looking forward to if you're not in it. Please say YES, you'll be my wife"...

Reading the note made Sincere cry even more, but the note he left somehow brought her peace. She removed all the rose petals off the bed and lay there holding the ring and note tightly. She clutched her pillow and cried herself to sleep. The next morning Shay was in the kitchen cooking breakfast, hoping Sincere would eat something.

The doorbell rang…

Shay wiped off her hands and rushed to the door, it was Tyra. She hugged Shay and asked, "Where's Sin, came as soon as I heard the news?" "She's in her room sleeping."

Shay helped Tyra get her bags, bringing them into the house.

Once her things were in the house, Tyra went straight to Sincere's room, kissed her forehead and said, "How are you doing honey, I came as fast as I could; have y'all heard anything?"

Tyra sat on the bed to comfort her grieving cousin. Sincere sat up, weak from crying, hugged Tyra, feeling confused and said, "I just don't understand who would want to hurt my Lex.

The police said, it was a robbery gone bad, but Tee my gut is saying it was something much deeper than that. I won't stop searching for clues until I find out who killed my Lex," Sincere hugged Tyra and began crying again... Tyra rubbed her cousin's back to comfort her then let her know she'd be with her through it all, she's not leaving until she's back on her feet completely.

It was the day of Lex's funeral and Sincere dreaded getting out of bed to face what she had to go through in the next few hours. She would be saying goodbye forever to her boyfriend, best friend, lover, business partner and most importantly her unborn child's father; Alex Cole Foster, a man that meant the world to her.

Getting dressed, Sincere moved slowly, she didn't want to deal with saying goodbye to Lex. She opened her closet door and began fumbling through her dresses. She found her royal blue Dolce & Gabana dress; it was Lex's favorite. She pulled it out, laid it on her bed, took a shower and then got dressed to go see her Lex for the last time.

“Sin the limo is here,” Tyra yelled to Sincere, who was finishing getting ready. “I'll be down in a minute Sincere yelled back, as she styled her hair, thinking how she wished Lex could’ve seen her. He would stop her in her tracks. They never got out the door whenever she wore that dress. She took one last glance in the mirror, took a deep breath, and then walked to join Tyra and

Shay, so they could head to Lex's home going service.

When they pulled up to *Walk by Faith Baptist Church*, cars were everywhere. There was a line from the church doors to the street. Everyone who was anyone came to pay their respects to Lex and his family. Sincere and the ladies got out of the limo to walk in the church with Lex’s parents; Mr. and Mrs. Foster, who were very heartbroken about their son being murdered. They walked up to the door. When Mrs. Foster saw Sincere, she gave her the biggest hug with tears in her eyes and said, “Sin sweetheart, I'm so happy that my son had someone who loved him as much as you did, and I can tell you, he loved you just as much. I thank God for leaving a part of my son here.”

She rubbed Sincere’s belly and they proceed to walk into the funeral. Walking in, the choir sang, “The battle is not yours,” People cried throughout the church. Everyone was saddened by the death of Alex Foster, a great man to all. However, no one felt the wrath of his death more than his mother and Sincere. His mother had lost her son and Sincere had lost her fiancé and unborn child’s father.

The home going service was a blur to Sincere; it was like she couldn't even remember what had gone on at the church, or the grave site. That was something she wanted to just forget ever happened, like she did a few other things in her past.

At Mr. and Mrs. Foster’s house, after Lex's wonderful home going service and burial, people showed their sympathy by bringing food, flowers, cards, or just their presence to say a few kind words of comfort. Sincere sat in a corner away from everyone, except Tyra and Shay, who never left their grieving cousin and friend.

Shay tried to get Sincere to eat something, when a hand touched Sincere's shoulder and said, "Sin, everybody's hurting right now over my nigga getting murdered, if you need anything just give me a call, I got you."

Sincere's body felt a cold chill when a hand touched her shoulder. She didn't know who it was until he spoke those words that made Sincere sick to her stomach. She turned around to see Aaron, Lex's right-hand man, standing there with cold eyes. His facial expression conveyed that he was sad, but his eyes said something different.

Sincere couldn't even respond to Aaron, she just said, "Excuse me" and ran into the bathroom where she threw up and began to cry? Sincere didn't like the feeling she got when Aaron came around, she's never trusted him, but Lex did, because they had known each other since first grade.

She figured Lex couldn't feel or see what she did about Aaron. Sincere hoped Lex's trust in Aaron wasn't the cause of them burying him today. She cleaned herself up before going back into the family room, where everyone was. When she sat down in her chair, Mr. Foster asked for everyone's attention, he had something he wanted to say. Mr. Foster wiped tears from his eyes with his handkerchief and began speaking.

Today is a day I thought I would never see. The day I had to bury one of my son's. A parent should never have to bury their child. A child should bury their parents, but the Lord works in mysterious ways and things aren't always how we want them to be. However, even in our time of mourning, we give the Lord much praise for giving us our son, Alex, for twenty-six years. He brought us much joy. Now the Lord has blessed us with a grandbaby coming in

October; our son Alex's first and only child."

Mr. Foster hugged Sincere and then walked off crying. After hearing that news everyone cheered and thanked God that Sincere was carrying a part of Lex, someone they loved dearly.

It was a little over a month since Lex had been murdered and the police still had no leads on who had committed this awful crime. Sincere tried to pick up the pieces, coping with life, living without Lex. It wasn't an easy thing, but she had to stay strong for her child that she carried. Tyra moved in after Lex's funeral to help Sincere run *House of Beauty*, and of course help with the baby when it was born. Sincere and Tyra looked at baby magazines to get ideas for a nursery.

Sincere would find out what she was having soon, so she wanted to get nursery ideas for a boy or girl. She wanted a boy so that she could name him after his father, but a girl would be nice too. She would still be a part of Lex, which made this pregnancy exciting for Sincere. She would get to meet the child Lex and she made out of love and that was a priceless feeling. Sincere reached over Tyra to get the bag of Doritos that sat on the end table. Tyra started munching on a Doritos and asked, "Do you think I'm going to get fatter than this Tee, be honest?"

Tyra tried to hold in her laugh and replied, "Yes you're four months pregnant and you eat like you're eating for three instead of two. You're going to be as big as this house, if you don't slow down."

Sincere gave Tyra the evil eye and stuffs more chips in her mouth. They continued talking and looking through magazines.

The doorbell rang…

Tyra jumped up to answer it. Sincere stopped her, saying, "No let me get it. I need the exercise before I get big as this house. "She laughed and answered the door.

She opened the door. It was two Roswell detectives; the short pale one asked, “Hi, are you Sincere Simmons? I'm detective Sporn and this is my partner Detective Powell. Can we come in? We have some information that we'd like to share with you about our investigation on the murder of your Fiancé’ Alex Cole Foster.”

Sincere, a little stunned, opened the door further for the officers to come in and tells them to have a seat. She took a seat herself, so she could hear what new leads were on Lex's murder. Detective Powell, a medium built, tall white man that looked as if he spent too much time at the tanning salon opened his briefcase, pulled out some papers and told Sincere the leads that have come in and what witnesses were saying. He put the papers down, looked at Sincere, who was sitting, thinking, “Is this all they wanted to tell me, they could have called.”

Det. Powell sighs, “Ma'am I have to tell you that Aaron Stokes, Mr. Foster's best friend has been picked up and charged with his murder, along with the two men that committed the actual crime.

Nineteen year old, Keronnie Morgan, and 21 year old, Willie Grey. Keronnie turned himself in last night and confessed to everything. They told us Aaron Stokes planned, plotted and paid them to kill Mr. Alex Cole Foster. Now, at least you and his family can have closure. The men that did this are in jail and will stand before a judge and jury.” Sincere thanked the detectives for coming by giving her the information on the case. She got their cards and closed the door and said to Tyra, “I knew that bastard wasn't to be trusted, he had my Lex murdered and it was nothing Lex wouldn't do for Aaron.”

Sincere shook her head in disbelief. She knew Aaron's eyes told a story of a man with a cold heart. Now, the only thing she could do was wait for the trial to watch Aaron Stokes could get what he deserved…life in prison.

Chapter 12

A RAINBOW AT THE END OF THE STORM

It's been six months since Sincere lost Lex. Life hadn't been easy living without him but the fact that she's having his twin son and daughter in a few weeks made her life worth living. She was ready to be a mother and finally see these precious human beings her and Lex made...

Sincere sat at her desk inside of *House of Beauty* when a tall brunette walked in with a heavy French accent and asked, “Excuse me, but do you only have women escorts, or do you offer men escorts for women as well?”

Sincere scooted her chair away from her desk smiled and answered, “Actually we're in the process of interviewing some men to escort and give massages to nice young women like you.” Sincere wasn't interviewing any potential men for this job, nor was this lady young, but one thing, Sincere wasn't was a fool, she knew expanding *House of Beauty* would make her establishment the hottest escort/massage parlor in Atlanta and with Lex dead and gone, two babies on the way; she had to make her money three-ways. She gave the French woman her card, took her information, and lets her know, she’d get back with her tomorrow morning. Sincere picked up the phone, dialed Tyra's number to let her know they have work to do and no time to do it.

“Hey Ms. Prego are you hungry?” Tyra said, when she answered, Sincere gave a short giggle. “Ah screw you Tee, no I'm not hungry yet. I'm calling because we need to round up a couple of nice looking men a.s.a.p., and we need these men like an hour ago. Look in my little address book, get Tavarious Campbell number, call him and tell him to meet me at my house in an hour. I have a business proposition for him. Tyra said ok, hung up with Sin got the address book and started to dial Tavarious Campbell for her cousin, "Yea who dis?" Tavarious answered.

Tyra paused a minute before saying, "Tavarious this Tee, Sin's cousin I'm calling you for Sin, she wanted you to meet her at her crib in about an hour. Can you make it? She said she had a business proposition for you."

Tavarious said, "O yea I can do dat for Sin, she my girl from way back and if she say its business I know Sin talking money I'm there. Give me thirty minutes, fuck an hour. Tell her whatever the plan, count me in, I'm down."

Tyra hung up the phone, called Sincere to let her know Tavarious said, give him thirty minutes, he'd be over to talk business. Sincere thanked Tyra and told her she'd be leaving *House of Beauty* in ten minutes and she wanted Tyra to meet her at the house too.

Sincere walked in the house, Tyra and Tavarious were in the family room, waiting for her to arrive.

"Gosh finally, Ms. Prego had waddled in the door, now we can talk business," Tyra said, laughing and clapping her hands joking with Sin.

Sincere big and almost nine months pregnant sat a bag of groceries down breathing hard and said, "Ha Ha Ha Tee, very funny. Yes Prego is here, but you'll still be waiting twenty minutes because I have to pee and if I don't put something more comfortable on, I'm going to bust out of this Donna Karan pant suit. So just bear with me a few more minutes babes."

Sincere waddled up to her bedroom to use the potty and change into a jogging suit, something she hated wearing, but being pregnant with twins, she had no choice although her pregnancy had been a joy. Sincere couldn't wait to get back in her dresses.

When she finished changing, Sincere asked Tee and Tavarious to meet her in the kitchen, she was starving, while they talked business she was going to be cooking so they could end this business deal with a meal, as she began dicing onions for her loaded stuffed peppers she looked at Tavarious and said, "Tavarious I asked you over here because I know you're a hustler like myself. I want to expand *House of Beauty,* making it for men and women to enjoy.

I had a French woman come in today, she'll be here for a month and she's willing to pay five thousand dollars a week for a male escort while she's in town. If we can get her to be a client of ours this could turn into something huge, bigger than I ever dreamed. If she's happy she'll let other people know about *House of Beauty;* it'll be like the domino effect.

The only thing is, I have no men employees yet, and Tavarious that's where you come in. You're an attractive guy that knew other attractive guys, how would you like coming to work for me at *House of Beauty* as an escort for the Elite of Atlanta?"

Tavarious looked at Sincere, eyes bigger than her belly and said, "Hell yeah, I'll come work for you, I'll even holla at a few of my nigga's for you Sin. We all can get a piece of this change telegram tela nigga it's the same as yo domino effect bit Sin," Tavarious nudged Sin and they laughed.

Tyra's face mugged up and she said, "Ok Sin, all that's fine and dandy like candy, but what all this gotta do with me?" Sincere bites a carrot and said to Tee, "Look heffa, I was getting to you next if you wait your turn momma; I got a job for you as well. She started telling Tyra she needed her to run *House of Beauty* until the twins are at least eight weeks old, that way she can spend time with them bonding before she comes back to run a business. Tyra agreed to help run the business so Sincere can prepare to be a momma to her and Lex's twins that were expected in four short weeks.

It had been three weeks since Tavarious Campbell had met with Sincere and in three weeks *House of Beauty* had already doubled its weekly profit. Sincere was very pregnant and very satisfied with the success of her business; she only wished Lex was still alive to see how well both *Peaches N Cream* and *House of Beauty* were doing. He'd be on top of the world being that he wasn't able to share this feeling with Sincere she would make sure she shined hard for the both of them. Anything else would be uncivilized; after all Lex was the reason Sincere had become so successful.

Sincere was due in less than a week and was getting bigger with each day that went by. The doctors have all been so surprised at the fact she was almost forty weeks pregnant and the twins weren't going to be premature. Sincere liked to think Lex was their guardian angel and he's keeping the babies safe inside her until it's time so they won't have to suffer in the world because they're already suffering having to be born in the world without a father.

October 14, 1997 was Sincere's due date and she wasn't having any contractions or anything. She was miserable because the twins have taken over her body completely; her stomach was so tight she couldn't even eat without getting sick. Her feet were swollen and looked like big boats. She just wanted her babies to come soon so momma could go back to being the diva she was.

Sincere lay on her couch flicking channels, watching her mother chase four year old Sami around her house. Neicy was supposed to be tending to Sincere but with Sami being an active toddler that wasn't happening.

The doorbell rings and little Sami ran to the door and said, "Who ringing that bell out there, not Sincere is leaping not sleeping."

Neicy moved Lil Sami out of the way and opened the door; standing there with a big pot was Lex's mother, Mrs. Foster.

Come in, Come in Neicy said to Mrs. Foster, greeting her with a hug and kiss on the cheek. "Let me take this for you, it sure smells good. Neicy took the pot and let Mrs. Foster know Sincere was in the living room watching TV while waiting for her water to break.

"Hi there sweetheart. I brought you some chili, maybe it'll be so spicy my grandbabies will run on outta there," Mrs. Foster said to Sincere, rubbing her belly, smiling.

"Oh m,a you have no idea how I want your grandbabies out of me and in my arms. I can barely move, my stomach is tight and as much as I love your chili I don't think the twins will let me enjoy it, but it's about to be fun finding out.

"Sincere got up from the couch smiling, waddling to the kitchen to fix her a big bowl of Momma Foster's homemade chili. When she reached the kitchen, Neicy had already fixed her a big bowl and loaded it with crackers, just how Sincere liked it.

"Aw thanks momma, you're always taking care of your pregnant baby girl," Sincere said to Neicy, scooting the bowl closer to her.

"You not the baby, I the baby," Lil Sami said, standing on Sincere's glass table with a frown on her face. Sincere *laughed* at her little sister who she loves dearly and said, "You're the little baby, I'm the big baby, now get your feet off my table Sami and have a seat so you can eat some chili, you lil booger."

After they all eat their chili and waiting for Sincere to go into labor the doorbell rings again, this time Mrs. Foster got it, it's Shay.

"Hi Mrs. Foster how are you doing? Is Sin having any

contractions yet? Shay said, taking off her jacket walking towards the living room to mess with Sincere.

Shay got to the living room where Neicy was putting Lil Sami down for a much needed nap, and Sincere lounged on the sofa while Tyra painted her toes.

Shay shook her head, "Oh no prego, those babies ain't never coming with you just sitting getting your toes painted, you have to move big momma. Tee and ya momma's being nice, but Shay here now boo let them toes dry then we're going for walk, we're going to walk those babies right out your tail."

Sincere rolled her eyes in her head and then said, "Ugh, Shay come on now, I don't feel like walking. I just want to sit and eat until my babies decide they ready to come meet their momma. U just chill out like the rest of us and eat some chili," Shay poked her lips out and cut her eyes at Sincere. "Okay, you're lucky both momma's are in the house or your tail would be walking no if's ands or buts' about it, mmm, I'ma eat some chili, but I'm not leaving until my niece and nephew are born, so how do you like those apples and oranges prego?"

Shay stuck out her tongue, waiting for Sincere's response. Sincere threw her head back, shaking her belly and said, "Lord please let me go into labor right now or Shay is going to work my last nerves."

Then she looked at Shay and said, "hmm, apples and oranges sounds good, I could go for an orange since you asked," Sincere laughed.

Shay went in the kitchen to make her some of Mrs. Foster famous chili and looked for pregnant craving Sincere an orange which she didn't find, but saw a tangerine.

"Well, this will have to do," Shay said, as she headed back to the living room, stands in front of Sincere and hands her the tangerine.

“This the closest thing you got to an orange Miss Piggy take it or leave it,” … Sincere twitched her lips, started peeling her piece of fruit and said “mmmmmmmmmuh, I guess I'll take it since you brought it, so thanks Florence.” Shay took a pillow off the loveseat and threw it at Sincere and they laughed.

Everyone had been at Sincere's house all day waiting for a contraction, her water to break or anything that was going to let them know the two blessings they'd all been waiting for were going to arrive; but nothing happened. Mrs. Foster did some cleaning for Sincere.

Neicy prepared her bag, before they called it a night and told Sincere to call them right away if anything had changed. They both kissed her on the cheek, and left the house. Tyra nor Shay left Sincere’s side. They wanted her to be as comfortable and have as much support as possible during this time; they knew it would be hard for her with Lex not around any longer.

The ladies waited patiently for the arrival of the twins for the next few days and nothing. Sincere had given up hope and just knew she would be the first woman on earth pregnant forever. She was tired of being in the house; that made her waiting seem even longer and had her very irritated.

So she told Tyra and Shay they should get out and do some shopping, something she loved to do. The ladies all got dressed and headed to *Arianna’s Mini Mall*. When they got to the mall Sincere told them she had to see if Shanyah's Baby Sensations had the double Eddie Bauer stroller she's been looking for forever it seems like.As they walk into Shanyah’s Baby Sensations Shay instantly spots the double Eddie Bauer stroller Sincere had been itching to purchase for her babies. “I got it I got it,Let’s go I need to do some non baby shopping” Shays lugging the stroller to the front of the store. Sincere looking at more baby things not paying

Shay any attention suddenly feels a warm trickle run down her leg she calls her cousin Tyra over then says “My water just broke let’s get my stroller and get to the hospital fast”. Tyra asks “Are you sure we can’t comeback for the stroller Sin?”. Sincere says loudly “HELL NO I WANT MY STROLLER “. So Shay pays for the stroller and the ladies speed off to the hospital to await the twins arrival. Pulling up Shay and Tyra jump out leaving Sincere in the car,After grabbing wheelchairs hurrying back to the car

Shay and Tyra looked at each other to see they both have wheelchairs. They laughed and put Sincere in one and wheeled her in the double doors, “*Mercy General Memorial Hospital...*

When they get to the labor and delivery floor a redheaded nurse with freckles, chewing gum asked, “Are you in labor honey, when is your due date?”

Sincere starting to have contraction now, took a deep breath, and said, “My due date was October 14th.”

The nurse said, “Ahh, looks like he or she wanted to come a lil late.” The redheaded nurse grins and hands Sincere papers to fill out which Shay filled out because Sincere’s contractions were coming a little harder at this time. Once Sincere signed the paper's Shay filled out, the nurse had someone push Sincere to a labor and delivery room.

In the room, Sincere got undressed and laid in the hospital bed so the nurse could hook her up to a few machines. They wanted to keep an eye on the babies during labor.

After the IV's were in and she was all hooked up to the machines the nurse said, “Ok Sincere sweetie, I'm going to check to see if you've dilated any. If you have a contraction, we'll pause until it’s finished.”

Sincere cut her eyes at the nurse and nodded her head so the nurse could check her.

"Oh these babies will be coming sometime today, you're three centimeters. First babies are tricky, they come when they want." The nurse pulled off her gloves, giving Sincere a smile, told her to push the call button if she needed anything or felt like she needed to push and leaves the room.

Tyra grabbed the phone to call her Uncle Sammy and Aunt Neicy to let them know Sin had gone into labor. She is at *Mercy General Memorial Hospital* and they can come out here. After hanging with her Aunt and Uncle, Tyra called Mr. and Mrs. Foster to let them know it was time, the babies would be coming soon. Both sets of grandparents had rushed to the hospital with arms full of teddy bears and other baby stuff for their new grandbabies.

Knock, Knock Sammy said, leading the other grandparents in the delivery room.

"Oh my sweet pumpkin, are the contractions coming pretty strong," Neicy said with tears in her eyes for two different reasons; her first born was having her first born which were twins and the other reason's because she couldn't stand to watch her baby girl in so much pain.

Rubbing her feet Mrs. Foster smiled at Sincere and said, "You can do this baby, and we're all here with you; be strong make Lex proud of you."

Sincere, still in lots of pain and at seven centimeters now, tried to give Mrs. Foster a smile, which turned into a frown because a very strong contraction came, and wanted someone to get a nurse, a doctor, or something; she was in pain.

The nurse rushed in, checks Sincere and said, "OK Sincere, that was a very good contraction a couple more like that and you'll be ready to push."

All the grandparents, Tyra and Shay got so excited they would finally be seeing what Lex and Sincere created together.

The nurse brought in Dr. Washington and a few more nurses who turned on a big lamp, two nursery beds, breaking down Sincere's bed.

Dr. Washington said, "Ok Sincere with your next contraction, PUSH! I'll count to ten, you'll stop and with another contraction we'll repeat these same stepped, you got it?"

Sincere shook her head and said, "OK, OK, I GOTTA PUSH."

Everyone in the room is yelling, PUSH, SIN PUSH.

Tyra with tears in her eyes told Sincere, "Keep pushing Sin, keep pushing til we see one of their headed."

Sincere heard they could see a head and began pushing with all her might, until a head popped out with a head full of curly jet black hair. The nurse suctions the baby's nose and mouth and told Sin to give one more push, then the first baby will be born, Sincere gave one big push, "It's a girl!

Everyone yelled, running towards the nursery bed forgetting there was another baby to be pushed out. Adoring the 5pounds 3oz 22inch beautiful grey eyed baby girl, just seconds old.

Sincere lying in the bed, still having contractions wondered what was taking her son so long to push his way down the canal. She was ready to see and hold both her babies.

The nurse looked over at the machine checking the baby's heartbeat and saw that Sincere's baby boy's heart rate was dropping.

She yelled, "Baby number two's heart rate is dropping," Dr. Washington said, "Hurry let's prep her for an emergency caesarean."

The room got quiet. Where there was just a room full of joy, it had turned to panic and worry that fast.

Dr. Washington told the family, Sincere wanted them all in the operating room, however, that's possible only one of them could be in there with her.

It was a pause and Neicy said, "Well I'm her mother I'm going in with my baby, I won't have it any other way."

Dr. Washington told Neicy to follow her so she could dress to be in the operating room.

In the operating room, Sincere looked so nervous all she could do was pray to God that he'd let her baby survive. She had already lost Lex, she couldn't lose their son too.

She thought in her head, "Lord if you hear me and I know you do, all I ask is that you get my son here safely. I lost his father, I can't lose him too, Lord just be with us, and Lex if you hear me, "tell the Lord to keep your son and I covered in the blood."

It was twenty minutes later, Sincere's son was crying a healthy six pounds eleven, ounce, twenty-four inches handsome green eyed baby boy, he too had a head full of curly hair.

Sincere and Neicy cried tears of joy when they saw her son because he looked exactly like his father. With the rest of the family waiting to meet their bouncing new baby boy. The doctor's and nurse's cared for Sincere and her new baby boy quickly so the family could enjoy the baby boy and baby girl together.

As they rolled Sin and her baby boy to the recovery room, the nurse told the family, they could have awhile to visit, but Sincere needed her rest. She had been through a lot. Natural child birth and a C-section all in one day; her body needed plenty of rest.

The family all gathered around the twins and congratulated Sincere on a good job with delivery.

Shay blurted out, "Hey wait Sin, are you going to tell us their names?"

Sincere with her eyes half closed and barely having a voice answered, “Yes I am, their names are Alex Cole Foster the second and Alexis Neh'cole Foster.

Everyone loved the names and the babies even more. They were fighting over who was going to hold which twin and for how long. Sincere half sleep wished Lex was there to share this joyful moment, while watching everyone take pictures and show her son and daughter so much love. October eighteenth, 1997 would be a day they all would remember.

Sincere looked up and whispered, “Yep, Lex baby you were right, there is a rainbow after every storm.”

Chapter 13

LIFE'S CHANGE

It's been eight weeks since Sincere had Alex and Alexis; she couldn't believe how fast they were growing and that it was almost time for her to go back to work, "Aww, my precious babies, momma will be off to work soon, I won't be home to love on both of you all day." Sincere said, playing with the twins on her California king bed.

Sincere enjoyed her time with the twins laughing and playing, when Tyra walked in the room with a big smile and her arms reaching out said, "Hey, hey share stingy, give me one of those lil hunnies."

Sincere giggled, kissing Alex's fingers and said, "Here TeeTee, you can take my little man, he still wanted to be up, my little princess is ready for her nap."

Tyra grabbed baby Alex while Sincere put Princess Alexis down for her nap. As soon as Sincere got Alexis off into a sound sleep the doorbell rings. Sincere sighed, looking at Alexis to make sure it didn't wake her and went to the door. She opened the door, it's her mother, her sister and of course Momma Foster. Both grandmothers' were bearing gifts.

"Are you going to help us with these bags or just stand there," Neicy said, as she shoved bags in Sincere's hands.

"Well you didn't give me a chance to lady," Sincere said smiling, looking at all the bags her mother and momma Foster had brought in.

"Where's the babies, where's the babies," a very hyper four year old Sami said, running through Sincere's house like she was outside?

Sincere gently pulled Sami to her and said, “Hey, hey, hey Sami come here, shhhhh, you have to be quiet because one of the babies are sleeping. If you want to see baby Alex you have to stop running and yelling, so you won't scare him.”

Cute four year old Sami in a little whisper looked at her big sister and said, “Otay, I not scared Anex shhhhh.”

Sincere shook her head and laughed at her little sister then escorts her to her bedroom where Tee and baby Alexis were watching Sesame Street.

“Oh my God, Tee you have my almost two month old son watching Sesame Street. I guess it's never too early to start a child learning,” Sincere said, as she picked Alex up so Sami could hold her nephew.

“Here you are Sami, your nephew, Alex; you’re an auntie at four years old.

Little Sami was smiling at the baby but couldn't take her eyes off big bird who was singing on Sesame Street.

“Okay Sami, I'll let you watch Sesame Street; you can play with Alex later. Sincere said, as she picked up her son.

Momma Foster reached her arms out for Alex. “Wait a minute, give Granny her baby, I missed both my babies so much.”

“Umm, Mrs. Foster you just saw your grandbabies yesterday,” Tyra said laughing at Momma Foster who was a very proud grandmother.

Momma Foster played with baby Alex when they heard Alexis start fussing in her nursery.

“I'll go get my pumpkin; I can't have her fussing too long, Neicy said, running to rescue baby Alexis out her crib.

They were all enjoying the twins when Momma Foster realized it was almost time for Sincere to go back to work. So she asked Sincere what she was going to do with the twins while running two businesses.

Grabbing diapers from the changing table in her room Sincere said, “Well, I've actually been interviewing nannies; Momma Foster gave Sincere a look.

Sincere rubbed Momma Foster's back and let her know, “I know I have you Momma Foster, but twins are a lot of work, I couldn't leave them with you eight to ten hours a day, seven days a week. I would rather hire someone that will help you out.”

Momma Foster never taking her eyes off baby Alex said, “Nannies are nice I suppose, I will keep the twins Monday-Wednesday and Thursday-Sunday, I'll keep an eye on the nanny.”

They all laughed because everyone knew Momma Foster didn’t trust her only grandchildren with a nanny until they were talking.

Sincere was enjoying the time with her mother and Momma Foster; however, she hadn't had any time to work on her figure since she’d had the twins. She figured this would be a good time to take a jog around her neighborhood park a few times.

She turned to Tyra and asked, “Tee you feel like jogging a few laps around the park, I need to get this body back right and you could run those three steak tacos off you ate last night.” Sincere, laughed then popped Tee with her towel.

Tyra laughed, looked at Sincere then replied, “Ah, you want to talk about me, now I didn't tell you to make the taco's so darn good, but it's on now Ms. Fitness I bet when we get to this park you get tired before I do.”

Sincere held her hand to shake on it, and then asked Tyra, “Okay so what we going to bet Ms. Steak N Shake?”

Tyra pulling her hair into a ponytail said, “If I get tired before you, I’ll change both twins’ diapers for a week.

If you get tired before me, you will have to pamper me for a week."

Sincere shook Tyra's hand and let her know it's a bet, then the ladies head to the neighborhood park for their jog. As they enter the park, it was people on bikes everywhere. The park was filled with cheering moms, dads, husbands, wives, and other family members for the bikers.

"Ah shoot, today is the bicycle marathon. But this bet is on," Sincere said to Tyra, as she took a sip of her water bottle, "Let's get it then girl, no time for water breaks," Tyra hit Sincere's butt and started jogging.

Sincere finished her sip of water and took off behind Tyra. The ladies jogged two miles, both of them tired but refused to give up, neither one liked to come in second.

Out of breath sweating hot and thirsty Tyra said, "Wait Sin, shit I'm tired, whew, girl I need a drink of my water, I give up you win."

Sincere out of breath herself laughed at her cousin sitting on a bench said, "Ahh, Tee I told you, don't let me having twins fool ya, because I'm still in shape, however, girl you gave me a run for my money. I'm beat, I was jogging thinking when is this heffa going to get tired."

The ladies laugh while they rest on the park bench watching the bikers ride pass.

"Well Tee babe you got a real shitty job ahead of you this week, changing all the twins' diapers. Do you need me to give you a week off from *House of Beauty* and *Peaches N Cream*, because changing all the diapers means ALL the diapers," Sincere looked at Tee with a smirk, trying not to laugh at her cousin.

"Ahh hell Sin, I need my week off with pay because Alex poops more than the average baby, you're right I gotta shitty job ahead of me this next week.

Oh lawd, why did I make that bet," Tyra wiped her

face with her towel and shook her head while wiping.

As the ladies get up from the bench to begin walking the two miles back to the entrance of the park, one of the biker's bike chains broke so he stopped right beside Sincere and began fixing his chain.

He heard Sincere say to Tyra, "Alright Tee, are you ready, let's make it up this hill?"

The man looked up because he didn't realize the two beautiful women standing there; he was so focused on his bike.

"I'm sorry ladies; I was so upset about my bike I didn't even realize you two beautiful ladies standing there. Hello my name is Michael."

The 6'2 honey gold skinned, salt n pepper colored hair, and hazel brown eyed man, said, as he reached his hand out to Sincere.

Sincere saying to herself, "this man is sexy, where had he been these last few months of my life," reaching her hand out and said, "Hello Michael, my name is Sincere and this is my cousin, Tee; nice meeting you. We see you're having a little bike trouble, do you need some help?"

"Naw, I got it, this will just have me behind in the marathon but I'll be just fine," Michael said, looking at his bike still dreading to fix the chain.

Sincere and Tyra head up the path when Michael yelled, "Hey Sincere how about dinner sometime, can I get your number?"

Sincere smiled and yelled back, "If it's meant for us to have dinner we'll meet again, until then have a great day. I hope you get your bike rolling again Michael."

"Mother's we're back," Sincere yelled, as she and Tyra walked in her door.

"Hey we're all in here, baby girl," Neicy yelled from the family room.

Sincere and Tyra walked in the family room where Neicy, Sami, Momma Foster and the twins were watching home videos.

Momma Foster wanted to make sure Alex and Alexis knew their father in every way possible, he wasn't there in the flesh but he'd always be there in spirit and in their hearts.

"Oh wow you guys started without me? I was supposed to video record Alex and Alexis watching Lex's videos. Look at Alexis, she acts as if she really knew what she's watching, as if she knew this is her father she's looking at on the TV."

"She does," Momma Foster glanced up from the TV to defend her two month old grandbaby.

Sincere shook her head at Momma Foster then went in her room to take a shower. She hated being sweaty. As Sincere turned on the water, she looked up at a picture of her and Lex on her bathroom wall, rubbed Lex's face, kissed it then said to herself, "Man baby how I miss you so much, not a day went by that I don't think of you, I miss your touch, your voice, everything about you, I know you would want me strong for our babies so I'll continue to do so, although it's hard, I'm moving forward each day to fulfill all our dreams. I love you Alex Foster, always and forever."

Tears roll down Sincere's face, as she washed the sweat from her body. Losing Lex still gave her stomach an awful pain and her heart a different kind of hurt; a hurt she'd never want to feel again.

After her shower, Sincere went to the kitchen to prepare dinner for everyone in the house. She thought it would be nice to have a nice dinner, and then watch some movies before she went to bed. She had a busy day the next day interviewing nannies for the twins, something she didn't want to do but was needed, if she wanted to continue having two successful businesses in the Metro Atlanta area.

CALL NOW BEFORE WE SALE OUT $19.95 IS ALL YOU'LL PAY FOR THIS SET VALUED AT$199.99. Sincere jumped up to the TV loud as ever with an infomercial on Stretches. She looked around and smiled to see Tee sleeping on the loveseat with Sami lying on her head.

Momma Foster was guarding Alex with her life as they're sleeping on the couch. Neicy and Alexis was cuddled together on a big soft pallet on the family room floor.

Sincere ran upstairs to her bedroom, grabbed her camera to take pictures of this priceless moment.

She's taking pictures of everyone sleeping when she heard Tyra's voice muffled, because Sami's little body was covering her head saying, "Sin you better not be taking pictures of this, and come get little Miss Sami off of me before she decides to have an accident in her sleep."

Sincere laughed picking her little sister up from Tyra's head.

"I already snapped at least seven pictures of this moment. Tee you looked cute with Sami's butt on your cheek aww."

Tyra throws a pillow at Sincere.

Sincere said, "Forget you Sin, and you better not get those pictures developed either hussie, I do not want pictures of Sami's butt in my face while we're sleeping."

"Aww, Tee stop being a party pooper, you know you guys looked cute; besides Sami is only four, her butt doesn't stink yet!" Sincere laughed while pinching Tyra's cheeks to make her laugh with her.

So Tee, do you want to help me interview some nannies for Alex and Alexis today? The first nanny is due here at 10am for her interview."

"Umm, do I have a choice? If I say no, you're gonna look sad until I give in, so yeah count me in. I want to meet them anyway; they're going to be in our house with our things with our babies I must check them out."

Tyra headed to her bedroom to lie down for a few more hours before she and Sin have to start interviewing potential nannies for the twins.

DING DONG the doorbell rings, Sincere looked at the time it's 9:45am; must be the first nanny she said to Tyra, as she walked down the hall to open the door, she opened the door and there stood a very pretty light skinned small petite young girl with hazel eyes with bright red dye in her hair and the girl said with a big pretty smile, "Hi my name Ta'Miya Manahand. I'm here for the 10 o'clock interview for the nanny position."

Sincere smiled, "come in Ta'Miya. I'm Sincere Simmons. I'm the one you will be working for. I have two month old twins Alex and Alexis, will that be a problem for you caring for two small infants?"

Ta'Miya looked Sincere in her eyes, "No I have no problem caring for two small babies. I'm looking forward to being a nanny; once I'm married I want to have at least five children of my own."

"Whoa five, you're a brave woman Ms. Ta'Miya. I think the twins are enough for me. I have my little prince and princess, it's been a wrap for me, but tell me a little something about yourself." Sincere said as she pulled out a chair from the dining room table looking over Ta'Miya's resume.

Ta'Miya clears her throat and began, "Well I'm eighteen, my birthday is July seventeenth. I'm a cancer, I actually moved here from New York {Manhattan} to attend Spellman, however I decided to wait a year so I can save more money of my own instead of living off my father's money. Daddy's money is very nice and very long but I think it's time I fend for myself, so daddy will be so proud of me."

Sincere put her hand up to stop Ta'Miya before she can speak another word. "Miya, can I call you Miya? Ta'Miya shook her head yes and Sincere began speaking again.

"Miya, oh my God when you sat down you reminded me so much of myself, and then you said, your birthday. We were born on the same day and I too am a daddy's girl. I know where you're trying to go in life TaMiya, and I'm willing to give you a try."

Ta'Miya jumped up and gave Sincere a big hug and smile to go with it. "Really, thank you so much, oh wow; my first job."

Sincere smiling and hugging Ta'Miya back said, "You are welcome. I need to check out your references and background because you will be caring for my babies. They are my world, and I can't just let anyone handle them."

Ta'Miya looked at Sincere reassuring her she wouldn't be disappointed.

"I understand exactly what you mean Ms. Simmons, you can trust me, I will love your babies as if they were my own."

Sincere and Ta'Miya shake hands as they're walking down the hall towards the front door. Sincere let's Ta'Miya know she'd be getting back to her right after Christmas {which was only a week away}. Then if everything checks out you Can start right after the New Year. Ta'Miya thanks Sincere again as she went out the door.

Thinking to herself, that went very well, not as bad as I thought it would be. Sincere headed to her office where Tyra was giving an interview to another potential nanny. She peeks in to see if they were wrapping it up before she just barged in.

She saw Tyra shaking the nanny's hand so that was her cue she could barge in now.

“Hello, I'm Sincere Simmons the woman whose children you’re interviewing to care for. Nice meeting you and your name is?” Sincere reached her hand out to the five foot tall grey/blonde haired bright blue eyed plus size woman in front of her.

“Hello Ms. Simmons, the lady said in a British accent. My name is Annabel. It's a pleasure to meet you. I read about you in the *ATLANTA'S STAR DAILY SUNTIMES* last week. I'm honored just to have had an interview in your home, oh and last but not least, congratulations on your award you will be receiving on New Year’s Eve at the *LOEWS HOTEL*.”

“Well, well, well, I see someone had done their homework on me,” Sincere said with a laugh, letting Annabel know she was flattered that she took the time to know so much about her and she would hear back from either Tyra or herself letting her know what the decision will be.

Tyra walked in the family room where she saw Sincere holding Alexis and making goofy faces at her. She sat beside her cousin and grabbed baby Alex then asked, “So Sin what's your thoughts on Annabel from what little time you had with her?” Sincere kissed Alexis on the cheek putting her in her swing. She then grabbed Annabel's resume off the table.

She glanced through it and answered Tyra, “I was impressed; she took time to find out who exactly she was applying to work for, and looking at her resume she is great. She is even a housekeeper as well, that's a plus in my book, beings that MiMi had been in our family many years as a nanny and housekeeper. UGH, I have a hard decision to make Tee. I like both ladies I met today, they both have high points that I like. Tee I'm going to hire both. Ta'Miya during the day 8am-7pm and I want to hire Annabel to be my live in nanny/housekeeper. She will be here as long as she likes. Ta'Miya I'm giving her a start in life making her own money so she can go on to Spellman in a year."

Tyra high fives Sin telling her she agreed with the decision she had made. Now they can focus on turning *Peaches N Cream* into a Dance Club/Lounge and move the girls to *House of Beauty* to do private parties. Tyra went in the kitchen; popped open a bottle of wine and poured two glasses. She returned to the family room and hands a glass to Sincere.

They hold their glasses up and Tyra speaks, "Cheers to us cuz, successful young black women, moving up in life's corporate ladder. It's a wonderful feeling. Thanks for including me in your dreams. Together we will continue to shine."

They click their glasses, "TO US."

Chapter 14

A NEW BEGINNING

It's NYE 1997 and Sincere is ecstatic about the award she will be receiving in just a few hours for the #1 HOTTEST NIGHTLIFE GENTLEMEN'S CLUB in ATLANTA from VEGASTIMES ENTERTAINMENT magazine. She's looking through her closet trying to find the perfect dress for her night accepting an award she and Lex earned together. Without Lex, there would not be a place called *Peaches N Cream* Gentleman's Club. Sincere would accept this award with pride tonight and she knew Lex would have been so proud of their accomplishment and success.

"Tee I need your help, hurry come quick," Sincere is screaming from her walk in closet so Tyra can hear her.

Tyra comes running down the hall from her room, rushing in Sincere's room with just panties, bra and her nylons on.

Putting her long diamond earrings in her ear, wondering what happened asking and looking confused, "What What? What's going on Sin, you ok?"

Walking out the closet with two dresses against her, Sincere said sweetly and calmly, "I'm fine Tee; I just need your help picking a dress for tonight. I was screaming before because I wanted to make sure you heard me, but it's good to know if I'm ever screaming, you will hear me and come to my rescue.

Next time Tee, have a bat or something in your hand just in case its danger once you enter." They laugh while deciding what dress Sincere should wear. They decide, it will be her all white custom made VERA WANG wedding gown with real diamond beading gently complimenting the front of her dress, she had redone after Lex was murdered.

"You really think I should wear this tonight Tee?" Sincere asked her cousin while looking in the mirror, holding the twenty-five thousand dollar dress up to her.

"Of course I do Sin true enough this was supposed to be your wedding dress, but tonight is also a big night for you and Lex. You're going to accept an award for something he started before he was tragically taken away from us all. Wear your dress Sin you're going to look amazing. Lex would want you to look beautiful tonight."

Tyra gave Sincere a hug and wink, and then walked toward the door to finish getting dressed herself before they hit the red carpet. Afterward they will celebrate the end of 1997 and the beginning of 1998.

"WOW princess you look absolutely gorgeous," Sammy said as he saw his oldest daughter walk down the stairs to attend her first red carpet event where she will be receiving one of the awards. Sammy was a proud father. He loved what his daughter was accomplishing without his help. She had done it on her own even though both her parents are powerful people in Atlanta; Sincere had made her own name in the big city.

As they pull up in the 1998 Stretch Limo Sammy had gotten just for his princess. People were everywhere taking pictures, cheering, throwing confetti, blowing horns, celebrating the New Year coming and the entertainment awards.

Sincere was the last one to step out the limo. She turned headed, looking flawless in her custom made *VERA WANG* gown. Her back was completely out. It was low-cut in the front, and fit just right, with a medium length train that ended the dress perfectly.

Entering the *LOEWS* hotel, paparazzi was taken

pictures of Sincere, yelling out, "Looking beautiful!" "What a dress you're wearing." The compliments and paparazzi followed Sincere to her seat. She felt like she was Miss America there to accept her crown.

The award ceremony went very well. It was almost midnight, so everyone wanted to get to the after party to bring in 1998 with their champagne glasses lifted and horns blowing.

Entering the after party, Sincere headed straight to the powder room to make sure everything was still in place.

Shay is right behind her, "Wait for me Sin, you may be going to look in the mirror, but I have to pee, girly watch out."

Tyra gave Shay a dirty look, "Gosh Shay, must you be so ghetto all the time? Can you vow to not be so ghetto in '98, please geez."

Shay with her dress half up running in a bathroom stalk laughed and said to Tyra, "Now Tee u know you can take the girl out the hood, but you can't take the hood out the girl.

I'm Shay thizzy forever biotch."

Sincere looking in the mirror shaking her head at her best friend and cousin telling them tonight is not the night to disagree on anything. Cut the crap! Let's party, because it's 1998. Coming out the restroom a 6 feet tall man with wavy hair, dark skin, and a big smile showing all his white teeth bumps into Sincere.

"Why excuse me beautiful. I guess I should watch where I'm going."

Sincere looked the man up and down, licked her lips and said, "Why I guess you should, if you had a drink in your hand my dress could have been ruined."

The man laughed, never taking his eyes off Sincere who he thought is the most beautiful woman he's seen in years.

"Let me introduce myself, my name is Vernon James, and what is your name beautiful?"

Sincere gave Vernon a smile with her green eyes then answered, "Hello Mr. James, my name is Sincere Simmons, nice meeting you and happy New Year."

As Sincere tried to walk off to start enjoying her night, Vernon gently grabbed her arm, "Hey beautiful I can't let you walk away from me that easy without giving you my card, hopefully you'll use it, and I'd love to have dinner with you sometime."

Sincere took the card and put it in her clutch purse and pulled out her business card and hands it to Vernon.

"Here's my card as well, if you want to take me out for dinner, you'll use the number that's on the card. Now you enjoy your night Mr. James, maybe 1998 will have something special in store for us, time will tell."

She walked off to join her family, leaving Vernon where he stood. All Vernon could do, was watch Sincere walk away as he thought to himself, "Damn I want that woman. I'm going to get her and once I do, she's never going anywhere, she'll be mine forever."

It's 4am and the after party is slowly ending. Everyone had had a wonderful time still drinking, taking pictures, and dancing being blessed to see another year. Sincere is on the dance floor with her father, Sammy when he told her he had to take a rest he can't keep up with her anymore. She thought that was strange because her father could dance all night long, however, they were busy all day so he needed to rest a minute she thought. Still on the floor Sincere feels a tap on her shoulder and looked back to see Michael the man she had met in the park last week.

"Hello Ms. Sincere, Happy New Year, I'm very pleased to be in your presence again lovely lady, may I have this dance?"

Sincere grabbed Michael's hand as Luther Vandross', *If This World Were Mine,* played as they danced. She loved the way Michael felt against her and he smelled so damn good. It had been so long since Sincere had felt this way. Her body started to tingle and get moist in placed she hadn't felt since Lex passed. As they danced slowly, Michael whispered in Sincere's ear, "This is the first of many wonderful nights ahead Ms. Sincere Simmons, I hope you're ready." Loving this moment because it had been so long since she's felt a man touch, Sincere said in a soft voice, "I'm ready and willing."

They danced until the DJ wrapped his equipment up and the night crew shut off all the lights except one. Even then Sincere and Michael danced to the beat of their own music. She hadn't known Michael long; however, to Sincere it felt like she had known him a lifetime and she wanted to spend every moment she could with this man.

They finally realized they were the only two left in the building besides the workers. Tyra and Shay who were fast asleep head to head on a small bench in the corner, they couldn't leave the *LOEWS HOTEL* without Sincere.

As Michael helps Sincere put on her mink shawl, she glanced at the clock on the hotel wall, "Oh my, Michael it's almost 6am we've danced all night, it's a shame it had to end so soon. It was 6am, but for some reason it still wasn't long enough."

Michael gave Sincere a smile and looked into her green eyes and said, "Who said it had to end, we can go have breakfast to end a perfect evening, but the start of an even more perfect day. My driver can take us anywhere you'd like to go. My limo is right outside."

He took Sincere's hand, so they can walk out the double doors of the *LOEWS HOTEL*, when Sincere paused, "Wait Michael, I almost forgot my cousin and best friend are on the bench sleeping. They were waiting for me. I have to wake them and get them home before I do anything."

Michael looked over in the corner where he saw the two ladies fast asleep; he laughed, and then said, "It's okay, its room for them to come too, if you like we can take them home first. They're welcome to join us, or they can finish their nap in my limo. They'll be safe. No harm will be done to you or those ladies while you are with me promise."

Sincere decides to bring the ladies along only because she had just met Michael, no matter how comfortable she felt with him she didn't need anything to happen to her.

As they pull up to *VINIECE'S FIDDLES*, one of the most popular placed to go for breakfast in Roswell, GA, Sincere tried to wake Tyra and Shay so they could join she and Michael for breakfast, however, it didn't work. Neither one of them budged, so Sincere walked into *VINIECE'S FIDDLES*, where they ate, laughed and talked for hours. They both shared so many things about each other. Sincere found out Michael is forty-five with three daughters, his last name is Saintjohn, and he's the president of *EDWARDS and EDWARDS BANKING,* the largest banking corporation in the world right now. He's originally from New York, he had a home in Atlanta as well in the *HAMPTONS*, and he is separated soon to be divorced after a twenty year marriage.

After hours of talking, they decide to end their morning breakfast to go home and get some much needed rest. Michael's driver drove the ladies home. Michael helps Sincere to the door, kissed her on the cheek, and then thanks her for a wonderful evening.

She smiled and told Michael, "No, thank you for an evening I will never forget."

She closes her door and headed to her bedroom, she slips out of her *VERA WANG* gown getting in the bed with only her panties and bra on, she thought it's time for a new beginning. Putting the pieces of her life back together, she falls fast asleep with hopes of dreams of Michael.

Chapter 15

TWO ALWAYS BETTER THAN ONE!

It had been one month since Sincere had let Michael into her life and he's absolutely amazing. Sincere hadn't been this happy in a while. She loved this feeling, between becoming a mom, expanding her two businesses, and meeting Michael, she was on cloud nine not ever wanting to come down. Although she's on cloud nine, there is plenty of work to be done. Sincere is having apre-valentine's day ball at *Peaches N Cream*, in two days and all of ATL is raving about it. Tickets sold out weeks ago and Sincere was wondering if even she could get in and she owned the place.

Riiiiing the telephone rings, Sincere answered, "*House of Beauty,* this is Beauty speaking how may I help you?"

A muffled voice on the other end said, "Yes my name is Tony Anthony and I'm calling to set up an appointment to have someone share a ravishing dinner with me and escort me to the *WINTER WONDERLAND BALL* as well the day before Valentine's Day.

I understand it's just a week away, so I'm willing to pay ten thousand dollars upfront for the most beautiful girl you have at your establishment. I'm told it's the owner of the building, a Ms.

Sincere Simmons. Is there any way I can have this beautiful lady be my date for this night?"

Sincere paused then clears her throat before she said, "Why Mr. Anthony although *House of Beauty* is very intrigued by your offer, Ms. Simmons isn't one of the escorts, she's the owner and I doubt if she'd even take you up on your offer."

Mr. Anthony then let's her know he is willing to pay twenty-five thousand dollars upfront for Ms. Sincere Simmons to be his date for this one evening. Although he didn't know he was actually speaking with Sincere, Mr. Anthony was trying to persuade whomever he could to get this date with Sincere.

After an hour of convincing, not to mention an upfront payment of fifty-thousand dollars, Beauty told Mr. Anthony she would have Ms. Simmons at that location on the day before Valentine's Day. It was now an official date and Sincere was very anxious to find out who this Tony Anthony was and she would soon find out.

KNOCK KNOCK, Tyra and Tavarious walk into Sincere's office; she's glancing over the budget for the *PRE-VALENTINE'S DAY BALL*.

"Hey toots are you working hard or hardly working," Tyra said laughing as she plops herself down in a chair.

Sincere looked from the paperwork, "Ha ha ha very funny Tee you know I'm a very hard working woman even when I'm sleep I'm working."

They all go over everything that still needs to be done and they have only two days until the event, As they're talking, Sincere is wondering if she should tell Tyra about the call she received from Mr. Anthony, but Tavarious is right there plus Sincere wasn't sure if she was going on this fifty-thousand dollar date with Mr. Anthony.

So she decided to keep it to herself and finish the final things for her upcoming event. Right as they were going to call it a night they heard a beep which meant someone had enter the building.

Tavarious went towards the entrance, it's Vernon. He shook Tavarious hand, and then asked if Sincere Simmons is available. Tavarious got Sincere. She is very surprised to see that it's Vernon and thinking to herself this man is very persistent, but smiled as she approaches him, "Hello Mr.

James. So what brought you in today?"

Vernon smiled, "Well I was in the area, so I decided to stop by and see how you were doing. I see you have a party of some sort going on in a few days next door at your club, would you happen to have a date for the evening?"

Sincere gave Vernon a sad face before saying, "Aww, unfortunately, I do have a date for that particular evening, Mr. James, and however, I don't have a date for tonight." She gave Vernon a seductive look with her daring green eyes and Vernon was like putty in her hands, like most men were once they looked into her eyes.

She told Vernon she'd meet him around 8pm in front of the *LOEWS HOTEL* where they first met. He agreed. They went their separate ways. Then Sincere rushed home so she could spend time with her babies, then get beautified for her night out with Vernon, whom she was interested in getting to know a little better.

Although she had been seeing Michael the past month, she didn't see any harm in going on a date. After all, she had no rings on her finger from neither man, nor was this the 90's. All women are keeping a spare in case the man she's dealing with went flat.

"Seven-thirty, shoot I'm going to be late," Sincere said as she got out the shower. She's dripped wet reaching for the phone to call Vernon and let him know she'd be a little late.

She dialed his number; he picked up, "Hey beautiful, you ready a little early, I'm pleased."

Sincere sighed, "Well u might want to hold off on being pleased, because I'm calling to say I'm running a little late. I'm sorry we'll make it a late dinner, how about 9pm?"

Vernon agreed to meet her in the bar at the *LOEWS HOTEL*. She hung up the phone, went in her closet, and started looking for something to wear. It's a chilly February evening in Atlanta, so Sincere figured some nice jeans and sweater would suit the occasion. She pulled out her Donna Karan fitted jeans trimmed in pink, her Donna Karan pink cashmere sweater and her multicolored pinks Zanetti heels from Italy. She was ready for Vernon and the cool ATL night air. As she was rushing out her room door she realized she didn't have a coat, she ran back in her room grabbed her charcoal grey leather coat with the hood and headed downstairs.

She went in Annabelle's room where she was reading Alex and Alexis a bedtime story which neither baby was paying attention to. At four months Alexis was putting her feet in her mouth and Alex was reaching for the toys in front of him, however, Sincere loved the way Annabelle cared for her twin babies.

Sincere reached down and gave Alex his kissed first then she got to Alexis and had to give Alexis' feet and mouth kissed, but she enjoyed every kiss she shared with her princess.

Walking out the door she ran right into Michael who was standing there with a dozen roses just about to ring the doorbell. Michael's eyes got big when he saw Sincere looking very pretty in pink.

"I'm sorry, are you going out? You look simply gorgeous baby; I was going to surprise you with an evening out. I'll take a rain check. I won't stop you, go out have a nice time, and be careful. Call me if you need anything. If not, just give me a call letting me know you made it home safely." Michael hands Sincere the roses, kissed her and walk towards his car.

Sincere is still standing there with her mouth a little open because Michael didn't ask where she was going or nothing. Just handed her the roses, gave her a sweet kiss, and told her to call. That made her want to call Vernon and tell him she needed to take a rain check and be with

Michael, whom she was really falling for but Michael had already driven away.

She got in her car, put her roses in the backseat, and drives off to meet Vernon. As she pulled into the *LOEWS HOTEL*, she glanced over and saw her father's car.

She thought to herself, "Hmmm daddy must be having a business meeting here tonight."

The valet hands Sincere a ticket and she precedes into the hotel's bar lounge area. Soon as she got in, Vernon is standing there with a dozen roses and a smile, "Wow you look smashing this evening doll face." He took her hand and guided her to a small table in the corner of the bar. Vernon thought if they were off in the back he could have Sincere all to himself without so many eyes gawking at her. They ordered drinks while they waited on the waitress to return with their order.

Vernon looked across the table at Sincere and said, "I want to take this time to thank you for taking me up on my offer for dinner. I really wanted to take you to do something you've probably never done before, or maybe you have but I'm going to open your mind up to a whole another lifestyle."

Sincere lifted her eyebrow, "Oh really are you Mr. James. I guess I can open my mind up to different things I'm looking forward to see what's in store."

They sit chatting with each other; however, Sincere wasn't opening up to Vernon like she had Michael. She wanted to get to know him better before letting him know any more than he already known.

Before they decided to call it a night Sincere excused herself to the ladies room. While heading to the ladies room, she saw her father at a table with a medium built Hawaiian looking woman with long black hair down her back.

She went over to the table speaking to her father, but giving the woman a dirty look. "Hello daddy, didn't expect to see you here, late business meeting?"

Sammy clears his thought, got up from the table, kissed Sincere then said, "Why pumpkin it's a surprise and pleasure to see you here, I'd like you to meet Ms. Konia Miles she's our accountant for our California dealerships. "Ms. Miles, my oldest princess Sincere."

Konia reached her hand out to shake Sincere's hand, "Hello Sincere nice to finally meet you, your father had told us all so much about you."

Sincere gave a fake smile to Konia while shaking her hand. "Yeah nice meeting you as well, unfortunately, I can't say the same because I've never heard your name before today."

Sammy saw the look in his daughter's eyes and cuts in, "Princess what brought you here tonight, are Tyra and Shay waiting for you at your table'?

Sincere answered quickly and sharply, "No I'm on a date and you daddy?"

Sammy grabbed the papers from the table, holds them up and answered, "Working sweetheart, what daddy always does.

Sincere said a few more words to her father then headed into the ladies room. While looking in the mirror Sincere is thinking to herself, "Hmmm if I didn't know any better, from the way Ms. Konia Miles hands were sweaty and shaky when I shook her hand I'd think her and daddy had something going. Daddy is in California two-three times a month and my father would never cheat on my mother, he loves her and his family too much to hurt momma."

Sincere then fixes her hair, touched up her lips, and walk out the ladies room door.

When she returned to the table Vernon is patiently waiting on her, "Hey I thought you got lost beautiful, are you ready?"

Sincere grabbed her coat, "No, of course you didn't lose me; I ran into my dad, he's having a business meeting."

They're waiting for the valet to bring their cars around when Vernon asked Sincere if he could take her to lunch tomorrow.

She said, yes. He lets her know, he'll call her with the details in the morning. They give each other a hug, and then end the night.

Finally the night of the *PRE-VALENTINE'S DAY BALL* at *Peaches N Cream*. Sincere is so excited because this event tonight will make *Peaches N Cream* and *House of Beauty* known everywhere, and there is no way but up from here. She was ready for whatever success it was going to bring her.

As Michael escorted Sincere into her ball, all eyes were on them. Sincere looked fabulous in her long black Gucci dress, low-cut in the front her back out with a long split that showed all her long luscious legs. Michael loved seeing how all the men's eyes popped out their sockets as he and Sincere passed them. One of the men they passed was Vernon, he envied Michael at this moment; he wanted it to be him walking Sincere in the ball arm to arm.

He thought to himself as he took a sip of his drink, "Michael u won the battle but I will win the woman."

Everyone who's anyone had come to show support and be with the one they loved for a night of romantic fun.

Sincere and Michael are enjoying each other's company when Tyra and Tavarious walk over, "Hey you two. Oooh Sin you're looking mighty hot tonight and I don't mean fever hot either," Tyra said admiring her cousin's dress.

"We have a damn good turnout tonight. That means a lot of paperwork for me Monday morning, can I get your help," Tavarious said rubbing Tyra's hand?

Tyra smiled and gently rubbed Tavarious's face and said, "Of course I'll help you. Is paperwork all you need my help with doing?" Tavarious gave a laugh showing all his white teeth, "For now yes, however, something else might come up and your assistance will be appreciated," Tyra gave him a wink to let him see she is ready, willing, and able to help him out.

Sincere noticing the chemistry between Tyra and Tavarious, she smiled on the inside. She was happy Tyra had her eye on someone other than Keke Millhouse.

Tarvarious was handsome, a hard worker, very motivated and she could see the two together. Sincere sipped her glass of Cristal Champagne then said, "I see you two have gotten awfully close working together, I'm happy for the both of you, and love can be a wonderful thing when you've found the right one."

Then she kissed Michael letting him know he was her Mr. Right. Way off in the back of the club Sincere didn't even notice Vernon was watching Michael and her the whole night.

If Vernon is determined to win Sincere's love, he had to think of ways to get Michael out the picture. The DJ plays LeVert's, *Baby I'm Ready.* Michael took Sincere's hand and asked, "May I have this dance?"

Tavarious and Tyra do the same as both couples are on the floor grooving to the music when Vernon comes from nowhere, "Excuse me, may I cut in?" Michael looked at him as if he was saying, "nigga who the hell are you."

Sincere with a shocked but angry face said, "Vernon what the hell you doing? This is Michael the man I told you I've been dating; don't do this here, not now."

Michael confused, not having a clear understanding on what just happened, walked off and leaves Sincere on the dance floor. Sincere looked at Vernon and told him he shouldn't have done that, and then ran after Michael.

When she got outside, Michael's driver was opening his car door. She stops him, "Baby wait. Where do you think you're going? Let me explain who he is, please hear me out."

Michael walked to the other side of his car, opened the door and nodded his head, and moves his hand giving Sincere the hint to get in. She got in, he followed after her, and they pull off, leaving her event.

During the ride, she looked over at Michael who is clearly upset with her and not speaking to her, nor looking at her.

She rubbed Michael's salt n pepper hair, kissed his neck, then said real seductive, "baby are you mad at me. Don't be upset, you have nothing to be upset about, he's nothing but an old friend."

She explained to Michael who Vernon is. He's very understandable, once he knew nothing ever happened between Vernon and Sincere.

Sincere rests her head on Michael as his driver drives them to *MOXLEY ESTATES* where he lives. Sincere is sort of anxious to see where Michael lays his head every night. As they go through the gate Sincere looked out the window to see them approaching a 7,000sq ft. home.

She looked at Michael, "Oh baby, this your home? You told me you were living comfortable, but baby you're blessed. This is more than comfortable, I love it."

Michael kissed her on her forehead, "I'm glad you love it baby, my goal is for one day it'll be ours instead of just mine."

They enter Michael's home. He told Sincere she'd

have a tour, later he had something he wanted to show her. He guided her to his bedroom, placed her on a mink bear skinned rug in front of the fireplace in his bedroom, then told her don't move, just lay there looking beautiful.

So she does, she closes her eyes and lays there. Michael is lighting candles, running bath water, and then Sincere heard Teddy Pendergrass singing, *Turn Off The Lights.* Michael gently took off her heels, then sliding her dress off, rubbed her body as he removes her bra and panties, picked her up, walked her to his bathroom, where he placed her in a bubbled filled tub and began washing her body. Sincere tried to say something.

Michael kissed her, then said, "Shh, don't say anything, just let me please you, just enjoy this moment."

He continued to wash her body, and then gently kissed it as he washes her.

Sincere feels her body temperature rising, tingling, but mostly getting very wet and it wasn't from the water either. Michael was making her body feel things she hadn't felt in forever. Sincere loved this feeling more than she loved her designer clothes.

When Michael was done bathing her, he picked her back up, placed her in front of the fireplace. Once more he put in an 80's slow jam CD that started playing Meli'sa Morgan's, *Do Me Baby*, and he started doing just that.

Sincere started rubbing her body down with hot oil. Sincere thought she was in heaven as she feels Michael's lips lick her toes; he licked and kissed her whole entire body, not missing a spot.

However, he did pay some placed more attention than others. Sincere was so extremely wet she feels her juices running down her leg and tried to wipe it. Michael wouldn't notice, although he did grab her hand, pushed it away then said, "No baby I got that, I want to taste all of u. Then began to lick her body fluids off her leg, then placed his face back in her hello kitty and eats Sincere as if she was a nice juicy piece of prime rib.

She loved every minute of it, as her body got warm and very tingly. She could no longer take what Michael was doing to her. Her body started to jump a little, then her legs start to shake beyond her control, she lets out a loud moan that could probably heard all through the 10 bedroom estate. She didn't care because the feeling she just felt, felt more than great.

When he rose he asked in his deep sexy voice, "Did you like that baby?" Sincere nodded, "Yes I loved it more than you could imagine;" they begin to kiss passionately. Sincere rubbed Michael's body as it pressed up against hers.

Then reached for his penis. When she got to it, she could feel right away Michael was no Lex, he was a lot smaller, but she didn't let that ruin the sweet moment. She gently placed Michael's penis inside of her, grips it with her muscles and begin to move her body with Michaels. He wasn't expecting for Sincere to feel so good, so he lets her know, "Damn baby you feel so good, it's better than I imagined, I feel like you're Eve and I've just enter into the Garden of Eden. Oooooo baby this is the best I've ever had, please don't ever take it away."

Sincere kissed Michael then he flips her on top of him. Sincere positions herself as if she was a jockey, she gripped Michael's dick even tighter, then rode him like they were in the Kentucky derby, and she rode him until they fell asleep with him still inside of her in front of the fireplace.

"Mornin Sunshine," Sincere awakes wrapped in a silk blanket and Michael holding a plate with French toast with fresh strawberries, cut on top, eggs, and bacon.

Trying to chew the bacon, Michael had just put in her mouth, she said "Aw, thanks baby it looked wonderful! Let me go get myself together then we can enjoy this wonderful breakfast you've made."

Kissing her lips Michael stops her, "Baby you're already together; the moment you opened your eyes, that's all it took, just eat your breakfast. I want you to be your natural self around me. I'm forty-five baby; a grown man. I know everyone woke up with morning breath and eye boogers and if I can't see pass that, I'm no good for you no way." Then he started feeding her breakfast as they eat.

Michael asked Sincere, would she love to see him off to the airport.

Of course she said, yes. Michael was making her fall more in love with him each time he was in her presence. Sincere looked at the time and realized she hadn't seen her babies since she left home last night.

"Oh shit, I'm trippin, you got me in another world. I have to come down for a moment."

Sincere grabbed her cell phone off Michael's nightstand, turned to him then said, "excuse me for a few minutes baby; I have to check on my babies."

Michael nodded his head then walked their breakfast dishes out the room. Waiting for someone at her home to answer, Sincere started poking around Michael's room to see if she could find anything linking him to another woman. She found nothing.

"Simmons Residence," Ta'Miya answered.

"Good morning! My My, are my two bundles of joy up giving you a hard time?" Sincere asked. Ta'Miya laughing, and then told Sincere, the kids were fine, she had just fed them and put them down for nap because they had been up since 6am.

Feeling a little bit better now she was talking to Ta'Miya about Alex and Alexis knowing their fine, she let Ta'Miya know she'd be home in a few hours.

She was seeing her friend off to the airport, let Annabelle and Tyra know. They share a few more before hanging up. She lays her phone down on the bed then walked into Michael's bathroom which was huge, at least thirty people could fit in there, Sincere walked around this bathroom thinking, "Who thought to put a fireplace in their bathroom," she looked to see if it was all ready to have a fire; she took the gold box down which contained the matches then she started the fireplace and got into the huge walk in shower, which six people could probably shower at once. As she washed her body, letting the water hit her at every angle, she was startled by Michael opening the shower double doors holding a plate of fresh fruit he asked, "Sorry baby didn't mean to scare you just wanted to know if you wanted more."

Water dripped from her body. Sincere licked her lips and gave Michael her come get me look then said, "Some more of what? Breakfast or some more of you?"

Michael took his robe off, got in the shower with Sincere, bent her over and kissed her back as he pushed his short fat penis inside of her. Sincere squeezed her muscles which made Michael feel like he had the largest penis in the world. She let out a moan which made Michael bend her over further and go even deeper inside her; she loved every stroke he gave.

The two made love, then washed each other's bodies clean. Michael got out the shower first. He told Sincere to wait while he got her a towel; he brought her the towel then told her he had a surprise for her.

Sincere gave him a confused look because she was thinking, "What does this man have up his sleeve now; the excitement never ends with him."

As she's drying her body off walking into Michael's room, on his bed laid three big bags; one from *NEEK'S NIGHTIES and MORE*. The second one from *CHRISTIAN DIOR* and last but not least, one from *TIFFANY'S*.

She looked at Michael and said, "Aww baby, what did

you do and when did you do it?"

Michael gave Sincere a smile told her to go ahead and open them up. I hope everything is to your liking. Not knowing which gift to open first, she opened the one from *NEEK'S NIGHTIE'S and MORE*. In the box, it was a 100% silk panties and bra set, in love with the first gift, she couldn't wait to open the second. It was from *TIFFANY'S*. She opened the first box; in it were 10 carat diamond earrings. Sincere's eyes got so big; they almost popped out of their sockets.

Nervous about opening the second box from *TIFFANY'S*, she paused and asked, "Michael, why you did this for me; and how you know my underwear size, I never told you that?"

Michael rubbed his hands through Sincere's wet hair, looked into her eyes and then said, "Sincere I never had a woman make me feel the way you do. You make me want to pay attention to every inch of your body, and last night as I took off your clothes, I looked inside of everything to know your sizes without asking you down to your shoes and had my assistant run and pick you up some things this morning."

He kissed her, then told her, "Now finish opening up your surprise," When she opened the second *TIFFANY'S* box it was a diamond tennis bracelet to match the earrings. Sincere was very happy, after all, diamonds are a girl's best friend.

Thrilled about seeing what was in the *CHRISTIAN DIOR* bag, she pulled out the first box; it was a pair of fitted jeans and a teal green see through blouse. She loved it! Smiling big and ripping the second box open which held a pink evening gown that had the stomach and back areas out. Sincere pulled the gown out and told Michael how much she loved it. He told her he wanted her to wear it on Valentine's Day night when he returned. She then opened the last box. In it was a pair of five inch heels that matched perfectly with the jeans and blouse. Glad she loved all her gifts, Michael told Sincere they must hurry so he won't miss his flight. They got dressed and then his driver took them to the airport.

As they pull up, Sincere let Michael know she'd be missing him this week, so he better call every chance he got and have a safe trip. Michael assured her he'll call as much as possible. He'll call her when he lands.

He kissed her then told her, "Be good while I'm gone."

She kissed him back saying, "I'm always good, don't you get into any trouble Mr.," They hug and Michael went off to catch his plane.

When she opened her door she heard both twins laughing, Annabelle singing and Tyra talking to someone. The cloud she had been on the last twelve hours had finally come down. She was home and it was momma time. She began walking towards the kitchen where she heard everyone, she went in with a big smile, "Hey hey, hey, what I been missing ladies?" Giving her Alexis, Tyra said, "Well I'm glad you decided to join us Momma." You didn't miss too much of anything, but a few calls from Vernon. But from the smile you have on your face you had a wonderful night, which means you have some tea. I want to hear it, and you already know don't leave out the sugar."

Tyra grabbed Alex and told Sincere to come upstairs; she had some tea of her own to share as well. Sincere grabbed Alexis's and Alex's bottles. Secures Alexis on her hip, and followed Tyra up to her bedroom. When they reached Sincere's bedroom, they placed the twins in their playpen and Tyra instantly start spilling her tea.

Which was she and Tavarious Campbell had sex, and he now was a resident living on the corner of good pussy, and making him cum fast, he was sprung just that fast. Tyra knew she had him wrapped around her finger.

She and Sincere laughed then high fived each other. Before Sincere could start talking about her night with Michael, the phone rang, Tyra sighed and told Sincere it's no one but the stalker Vernon.

He had been calling all night, nonstop, Sincere picked up the phone, "Hello."

Vernon sounding upset said, "Yeah Sin, I see you finally decided to come home after a long night out."

Turning up her nose Sincere yelled sweetly at Vernon, "Look Vernon where I was last night, or when I returned home is irrelevant. Anyway I heard you've been calling me nonstop. How can I help you Mr. James."

Vernon apologizes to Sincere for coming at her sideways, and then asked her if she can please meet him at the lake in *JERRON TRAILS*. She agreed to meet him there in a few hours, and then she hung up the phone.

Sincere noticed the look Tyra was giving her, as she hung up the phone.

So she asked, "What Tee, why are you looking like that, I know you have something to say."

Tyra scratched the back of her head, took a deep breath then said, "Sin, I don't know Vernon very well, but something about him spells trouble to me, you better be careful with him he might be a psychopath underneath all that fine piece of man."

Sincere convinced Tyra she'd be fine, she wasn't planning to get serious with Vernon, Michael had her nose wide open and she couldn't wait to see how much more open he can have her especially after last night.

Sincere and Tyra finished sharing details about their evenings, when Trudy an employee at *House of Beauty* called with a message for Sincere, saying a Mr. Tony Anthony called saying he had to cancel his date and needed to reschedule it for three weeks from the original date planned.

Sincere took down the info, hung up the phone and spent time with the twins before she went to meet Vernon at the lake. As she changed her clothes because she refused to meet Vernon wearing all the gifts Michael had just given her.

She couldn't help but to wonder, "What the hell Vernon had up his sleeve, there was nothing except huge million dollar yachts and houseboats in *JERRON TRAILS* and it was a too cold this evening for a boat ride."

She was dressed and ready to impress as she walked out her room door, she went into the family room where Annabelle was watching a purple dinosaur named Barney on TV. She bent down, kissed the twins and told Annabelle she'd be home by eleven. Sincere drove off to meet Vernon at *JERRON TRAILS*.

Chapter 16

IS THE GRASS GREENER ON THE OTHER SIDE?

JERRON TRAILS is in big bold gold letters as Sincere entered the gates, she's driving down a rocky trail until she comes to a second set of gates that led to a huge parking garage.

When she entered the second gate, Vernon was standing right in front waiting for her with a white rose in one hand and waving thee other towards an empty space in the garage. Sincere parked then got out of her car, fixed her shirt, rubbed her lips together, and took a deep breath, then walked towards Vernon who's standing there with a big smile.

He handed her the rose, kissed her cheek then said, "I'm so pleased to have the pleasure of being in your presence once again Ms. Simmons, and let me add you're looking smashing this evening."

Sincere gave Vernon a partial hug then thanked him for the rose. Vernon asked her to take his hand as he led her down a trail made of cobblestone.

As they're walking, Sincere noticed the cobblestone trail is now turning into a small bridge made of marble, and they are now surrounded by nothing except water, huge million dollar yachts and houseboats.

Sincere sniffed her rose, and as they're walking, she turned to Vernon then said, "I'm impressed Mr. James, I didn't know what to expect with you, but this is nice. I've always wanted to see what makes people buy a houseboat in *JERRON TRAILS*, now I know it's beautiful and peaceful, but most importantly; it's a complete home, only sitting on water. I don't know if I could do the living on water thing though."

Vernon chuckled and looked at Sincere, points straight ahead and said, "Welcome to my getaway place, my houseboat is your houseboat," He then took Sincere's hand and they walk into the houseboat.

When entering Vernon took Sincere's jacket, placed it on the sofa and told her to make herself comfortable and he'll be back in a moment. Sincere took a seat on the leather chair she was standing beside while Vernon went into the kitchen. In the kitchen, Vernon pulled out a bottle of Rosé, he had chilling. Pours two glasses, hands Sincere a glass, and then asked her to follow him up top of the boat. Sincere grabbed the thick quilt laying over the loveseat, took Vernon's hand, and they walk up some stairs leading to the top of the houseboat.

Reaching the top, Sincere was taken away by the beautiful view of the stars that were shining so bright and all the lights from the yachts and other houseboats and the big buildings of downtown Atlanta looked breathtaking! She felt as if she could see all of Atlanta from up there, she took a seat on a small leather bench, sipped her Rosé, tapped the space next to her and told Vernon to have a seat.

Vernon sat next to her, tried to kiss her, but Sincere pulled back, and then explained to him that even though she's not fully committed to anyone, she had been seeing someone for almost two months and she was really falling for him, so she didn't want anything coming between what they have been trying to build. Vernon asked if the person she was speaking about the guy she was with at her party.

Sincere nodded, then Vernon gently touched Sincere's face, then let her know, he's not trying to come between anything she had going on with the old timer. He just wanted her to keep her mind and options open, give him a chance to prove himself as well. Sincere agreed to give Vernon a chance. She told him Michael will be gone for a week, so she will have some time to spend with him, but she can't promise him she would stop seeing Michael, but she was willing to give him a chance and see what he was about; the two click champagne glasses.

They begin talking and opening up to each other. Sincere told him about how her fiancé was murdered by his best friend, and she is now a single mother of twins. Vernon told Sincere how his father was murdered in front of him and his mother when he was three years old, and how his mom turned for the worse. She had gotten on drugs heavy after that, which landed him in foster home after foster home, being abused in ways people could only imagine, until the James family adopted him at eight years old. They changed his life gave him a wonderful home he got a good education.

He told Sincere, how thankful he was because he probably would have been dead or in prison, not sitting there with her if it wasn't for William and Marla James. Teary eyed by his story, Sincere kissed Vernon and told him, she's so sorry he had to endure so much the first years of his life.

Her heart went out to him, and she was happy the James family rescued him from a life of trauma.

She then nudged him and said, "You're a prime example that you can't always judge a book by its cover, you're a survivor."

They wrap themselves in the quilt Sincere brought up, then continued to talk and sip Rosé. Sincere felt so warm next to Vernon, she could stay wrapped in his arms forever, lying on his shoulder, she thought to herself, "James James William James," she popped her head up from Vernon shoulder then asked, "William James is your father? The William James of *JAMES and SON MOTORS.*

Sincere gave a sly smirk then continued, "He's my daddy's competition, *SIMMONS and SIMMONS* is the largest, and however, your father is our competition.

Vernon laughed loudly, putting his arms around Sincere. Then told her he doesn't want business to come between them. He wanted to be a part of her life, not just the son of William James. He kissed Sincere then the two cuddled back up and enjoyed each other's company until Sincere realized it was getting late.

She told Vernon she had a lovely evening but she had to call it a night. Not happy the night had to end; however understanding about it, Vernon walked Sincere back inside the houseboat put on her jacket for her then walked her to the parking garage to her car.

When they reached her car Sincere gave Vernon a big hug then gently kissed him on his cheek and attempts to get in, but Vernon had other plans. He grabbed Sincere's arm, pulled her close to him and start kissing her passionately, rubbing his hands all over her soft body Sincere is pushing away, but couldn't help kissing Vernon back, she said, "Wait Vernon baby, I have to get home, all this is just too soon."

Vernon not paying her any attention picked her up, placed her on the hood of her car gently pulled her jeans down then started tasting Sincere. She was pulling back, until Vernon's tongue touched a certain spot.

In that moment, she threw her head back and enjoyed what Vernon was doing. He told her he liked eating late, but this isn't what she had in mind.

Putting his face and tongue more in between Sincere's legs tasting all her sweetness, he's mumbling not even coming up, he said "Ooooooo Sin baby, you taste so damn good and smell so… I can stay down here forever," and that he tried to do.

Vernon had a picnic on the hood of Sincere's car, and

she was the food in his wooden basket. When Vernon finished his midnight snack, he wiped his mouth, and then told Sincere he never knew a woman could taste so sweet. She hopped off the hood of the car leaned over, then whispered in his ear, "and you never will." She gave him a wink, and then kissed him on his cheek, hopped in her car and drove home.

When she walked through her door she headed straight to her bedroom to take a hot shower, while washing her body she thought, "Wow, no man had ever ate me out two hours non- stop; this man had to have a battery in his mouth."

Her body still very wet (not from the shower either), her legs still shaking, all Sincere could do as she showered was think of what Vernon just did and how she wanted him to do it again. Stepping out the shower drying off, she realized she didn't check on her babies when she came through the door. She grabbed her robe then walked down the hall to check on Alex and Alexis.

When she got to Alexis's room, she was sound asleep. She kissed her, and then headed next door to Alex's room where he was wide awake, making noises at the mobile above him that's connected to his crib.

Sincere laughed, then shook her head, picked up Alex from his crib giving him some kisses, she said, "What is momma's lil man doing up, were you waiting on momma Lil Lex?"

Alex is jumping, giving Sincere a big smile with giggles, as if he was saying, "Yes momma, I was waiting for you."

Knowing she'd be up for a while, Sincere took Alex to her room, then went to get Alexis, brought her to her bedroom as well, placed her on her bed next to Alex who is fighting his sleep, she took off her robe slip into her nightgown then got in the bed with her twins holding them close to her until she and baby Alex falls asleep.

Waking up the next, with Alex arm over her eyes and Alexis trying to make her way to join him Sincere scooted Alexis closer so she and her babies can have their morning playtime. She spends the next hour tickling, kissing, and making funny faces with the twins.

When Ta'Miya comes in laughing because Sincere is cleaning Alexis's nose, while trying to stop Alex from grabbing Alexis's hair.

"Need some help?" Ta'Miya asked, while picking Alex up, Sincere looking up from cleaning Alexis nose, thanks Ta'Miya then said, "Whew, you're a lifesaver, I couldn't get the boogers out Lexie's nose, without Lil Lex pulling her hair. I know they're babies but at times, I swear they get jealous if I give one more attention than the other."

Sincere sighed, "Boy, do I, and two.

Reassuring Sincere things won't be that bad Ta'Miya, began getting Alex ready for a bath, then told Sincere she's going to take the twins for an outing for the day if it was alright with her. Sincere was delighted by the offer, hopped off the bed and began to get Alexis dressed.

In the middle of dressing, Alexis Sincere's cell phone rings, it's Vernon.

As soon as she answered, he said, "I hope you're ready for day two, I have something special planned for you so can you get a sitter for the night?"

Sincere hesitated for a second before she answered, "Yeah sure, I can do that, but can I ask where we're going?" Vernon told her it's a surprise, he's not telling her, but she'd be in good hands and returned home in one piece like he got her; then told Sincere he had a dentist appointment in an hour if she could meet him at his house in *HUNTLEY HILLS* . He gave her the address and let her know he'll be waiting and he couldn't wait to see her.

When she hung up the phone Sincere got a nasty feeling in her stomach because she hadn't been to *HUNTLEY HILLS* since she was raped by Kevin Millhouse. This was clearly a place she didn't want to go, however, she had moved on, pushing the rape in the back of her head, so she wasn't going to let it interfere with what she had going on in her life now.

With Alex and Alexis dressed ready to hit the road, Sincere gave them plenty of love before helping Ta'Miya get them in the car. As they're strapping the twins in, Ta'Miya let's Sincere know that she had planned on the staying overnight if she didn't mind. She wanted to give Annabelle a break from the nightshift.

Sincere surprised Ta'Miya even offered to be with the twins overnight, gave Ta'Miya a hug then told her she's the bes,t then watched Ta'Miya drive off with her babies.

Going back into the house Sincere heard the house phone ringing. She's running to the kitchen to answer it, she picked it up breathing heavy from running,

"Hello".

"Baby is this you" Michael said, on the other end of the phone.

"Yeah baby it's me. I was running trying to get the phone before it stop ringing."

"Oh ok I was wondering, because you were sounding like you were out of breath there for a minute."

Sincere gave a little giggle then told Michael how much she missed him already and could he rush a few of his meetings to get home to her sooner than planned. Michael let her know he hasn't stopped thinking about her since he left and he would see what he could do about coming home a day or two early. The two talk awhile longer until Michael had to prepare for a meeting; they say their goodbyes then hang up.

Hanging up the phone Sincere felt bad because Michael's preparing for meetings and she's preparing to meet Vernon, she looked in the mirror then said to herself, "I shouldn't be doing this to Michael, he is such a nice guy, but then again what Michael doesn't know won't hurt him; after all, when the cats away the mouse will play."

With that being said, she took a shower, put a short dress on for easy access just in case Vernon wanted to dine in again, then headed to *HUNTLEY HILLS* to see what Vernon had in store for her this time. As she entered the gate to *HUNTLEY HILLS* she began to get nervous because she's approaching the Millhouses home, a place she never wanted to return. She tried to calm her nerves before she reached Vernon's.

When she got to Vernon's home she saw there were two cars already parked. She thought to herself, "Hmm, someone has company," then looked in her rearview mirror, glosses her lips, and stepped out the car walking towards Vernon's front door.

She rings the bell, Vernon answered, wiping his hands, telling Sincere please come in. I'm in the kitchen having my private chef help me prepare us a nice dinner that isn't ready yet, but make yourself at home while I pour you a glass of wine. Sincere got comfortable on his sofa while she waited for her glass of wine. As Vernon is pouring the wine, Sincere glanced up at the picture above the fireplace, it's a beautiful oil painting of a woman and her son; they both look so sad in the painting, Sincere wondered who were they and why they looked so sad.

Coming into his living room holding the wine, Vernon saw Sincere staring at the painting. He hands her a glass then said, "I see you are checking out the painting of my real mother and I that was taken the day of my father's funeral; it was the only picture I had of my mom, so a few years ago I had someone paint me this portrait to go above my fireplace."

Saddened by the story behind the portrait Sincere sipped her wine, and told Vernon, how lovely it was and his mom was beautiful. The two sat on Vernon's sofa watching TV and drinking wine, until Vernon's chef came in saying, "Mr. James, your dinner is served, hope you two enjoy your meal."

Vernon took Sincere's hand, and then walked her to his dinner room where the chef had candles burning, soft music playing, and a delicious looking meal spread out on the table. Pulling her chair out for her Vernon asked Sincere to join him for dinner. They sit down to enjoy a lovely meal and conversation Vernon had Sincere laughing for hours before he finally asked Sincere to follow him back into his living room but this time he had her sit on his piano bench so he could play his black baby grand piano for her.

He gave Sincere a kiss, and then started to sing and play Luther Vandross's *Superstar* to her. Stopping playing the piano but still singing, Vernon placed Sincere on top of his baby grand caressing her body, he stops singing to say, "Damn girl, looking at you in this dress makes my mouth water; you're giving me a sweet tooth and the dentist told me to stay away from sweets, but fuck it, I'm about to get a cavity."

He lifted Sincere's dress up, pulled her panties to the side then had his dessert, satisfying his sweet tooth. Sincere, moaning and moving her body, pushing Vernon's head further between her legs, grabbing his ears telling Vernon she wanted him to touch her on the inside with his penis.

Enjoying tasting her juices flowing into his mouth Vernon continued to lick Sincere until she begged him to stop. Vernon came up for air, then gently picked Sincere up, carried her to his bedroom, lays her on his bed then he began to take his clothes off. Sincere is licking her lips as she watched Vernon undress.

Her body got hotter just by looking at him, she told him, "Hurry up or do you need some help getting those boxers off?"

She rose from the bed, grabbed Vernon's boxers then snatched them off. What she saw she wasn't prepared for and she got nervous before she knew it she said, out loud, "Oh my God, is that your dick hanging down to your knee, oh my gosh it can't be real, what have I gotten myself into?"

Sincere then backs away from Vernon, but he climbed in the bed next to her, kissing her and said, "Don't worry baby, I won't hurt you with it. I'm not here to hurt you; my job is to please you. I'll be gentle, if it starts to hurt, I'll take it out because the last thing I want to do is hurt something that is so damn good."

He started to kiss her body, relaxing her, before he put his twelve inch penis inside of her. Sincere was nervous; however, she still opened her legs and let Vernon fill her with his love, all night long.

The next few days for Sincere with Vernon had been unbelievable the two had been fishing, bowling, go-cart riding, playing pool, ice skating and not to mention Vernon had been dining in three times a day, breakfast, lunch, and dinner. Sincere was like a drug that Vernon sure had to have and Sincere didn't mind giving him his daily fix.

Kissing Sincere on her neck, Vernon told her he hopes this week doesn't have to end. He wanted to be the one she went to bed with at night, and the first face she saw when she wakes in the morning, he was falling for her and he didn't want it to end.

Not knowing what to say about what Vernon just said, Sincere asked Vernon if they could finish their conversation inside the restaurant. They were sitting outside of what was one of Vernon's favorite places to go when he came to the Westside of Atlanta. It was a nice restaurant on the corner of Clark Dr. and Gulley Pkwy, the sign said, in big bold black letters *ALICE HOMECOOKIN'*.

Sincere kept her body in shape; however, she loved to eat. She couldn't wait to see if *ALICE HOMECOOKIN'* was all that Vernon had been raving about. They walked in and Sincere couldn't believe how long the line was and almost every table was taken. She said to herself, "This Alice must be the best cook around these parts, these people in line as if she's giving away free food."

Sincere looked at Vernon, gave him a smile then said, "You might know a little something about good food Mr. James, this place is packed like a can of sardines and it smells so good I just want to sample everything."

Vernon laughed then said, "Smelling good is nothing when you taste the food you'll never go anywhere else for soul food Ms. Alice is the best cook in Georgia, but from Mississippi and I've been eating her cooking since I was a small kid my first foster mother brought me here I've been coming ever since."

Before Vernon could say another word, a short medium build light-skinned lady with thick black hair and big round cheeks comes from behind the counter, gave Vernon a big smile then hugs him, her name tag said, Alice.

Vernon hugs Ms. Alice tightly and she popped him with her towel, and then said, "Why haven't you been in here the last few weeks. Vernon we been missing you around here boy, come sit yourself down at one of these free tables, you're like my grandson, you don't wait in line when you come to my place."

Ms. Alice's placed them at a table, pulled out her pen and pad then asked them both what they were having Vernon told her ,"Ms. Alice give us the works; give us a little of everything you have today," Ms. Alice smiled, then said, "You got it, everything coming right up."

Ten minutes later Ms. Alice returned with three waiters they placed another table beside Vernon and

Sincere's table. Then began placing fried chicken, meatloaf, fried catfish, smothered pork chopped, greens, cabbage, mac n cheese, sweet potatoes, dressing, potato salad, black-eyed peas, dirty rice, the list went on.

Sincere's eyes got big from all the food they were putting in front and beside them, she looked at Vernon and said, "Baby when I said, I wanted to try everything I didn't really mean it silly, but I am going to try to stick a fork in everything Ms. Alice had brought."

As the waiters finish putting the feast out for the two of them, Ms. Alice stood there as if she's waiting for Sincere to take a bite of something on the table. So Sincere began fixing her a plate, she stuck her fork into the dressing, took a bite, rolled her eyes in her head then said, "Mmm, Ms. Alice, Ms. Alice, Ms. Alice ma'am, this is the best turkey dressing I ever had, oh my God, I have to taste this mac n cheese, Mmm, oh lawd Ms. Alice, this is very good too, how did you learn to cook like this?"

Ms. Alice gave a loud chuckle, touched Sincere's shoulder, then said, "Baby when you raised eight kids of your own and have over forty grandkids and great grandkids running in and out your house daily like I do baby, cookin comes natural, plus I always loved keeping my family close by sharing big Sunday meals together."

Still stuffing her face Sincere gave Ms. Alice thumbs up for all the good food she had prepared. Ms. Alice gave Vernon a pat on his back, tell him don't make it another few weeks before she saw him again and looked at Sincere told her don't be a stranger and she can't take the credit for the banana pudding and sweet potatoes she was scarfing down, those two things were her best friend Jessie B recipes.

Enjoy it all! Then Ms. Alice went back to running her restaurant.

Sincere and Vernon sit inside *ALICE'S* for hours talking about their different upbringings, their likes and dislikes and where they wanted to be in the next five years. When that conversation arose Vernon took the opportunity to ask Sincere once again would she like to take this friendship further.

She'd been trying not to answer Vernon all day, but now she can't avoid him any longer, she took a sip of her sweet tea, looked at Vernon then said, "Yes Vernon, I'd love to."

Sincere knew what she just said out her mouth is not what she meant, she loved Michael, that's the man she wanted to take things further with, but the look in Vernon's eyes had her hesitant to say no to him. She's thinking to herself, "Oh my God, what have I just said," Vernon, happy his mission was accomplished.

Getting Sincere to want him he thought to himself, "I got her right where I want her, she's mine forever. I'm never letting her leave me," then he rubbed Sincere's hand and asked, "If she ready to leave, because he wanted to celebrate with a little dessert and what he wanted... *ALICE'S* didn't have.

Sincere still thinking what had she done, but had become so infatuated with the way Vernon was giving her pleasure, she just picked up her purse, took Vernon's hand and they leave for *HUNTLEY HILLS*.

When they arrive to Vernon's home, he asked Sincere would she join him in his Jacuzzi room and before she could even answer, Vernon was already taking off her clothes then opening the doors to his Jacuzzi room.

He got in the warm Jacuzzi then said to Sincere "Girl, come get your sexy ass in this tub."

Sincere took of her bra got in the Jacuzzi. Vernon didn't waste any time having his sweet dessert, his tongue moving faster than a tornado ripping through a town had Sincere going crazy; she's moving away from him not even realizing she is, she said, "Oooo damn slow down cookie,"

cookie was a nickname she had secretly given Vernon.

It was short for cookie monster, because he loved munchin on her cookie. Vernon rose up laughing, "Did you just call me cookie?"

Sincere ashamed she said it out loud, gave an innocent smile saying, "Yes I did baby, that's my nickname for you, cookie, because you're my own personal cookie monster. I hope you're not upset about it."

Vernon shook his head no, then dives face first into her cookie, doing it better than before; he was gonna live up to his name and Sincere was loving it. After he was finished, he turned Sincere and had her raise her butt up then started rubbing her clit with his fingers as he massaged her vagina's hole with his large penis relaxing her for what he was about to do. Vernon then shoved his penis inside of her.

Sincere lets out a loud scream, he kissed her back saying, shh, relax I'm going to make this feel real good, just let me all the way in. Sincere relaxed and let Vernon do what he wanted; he was hitting spots she didn't know she had and the deeper he went the wetter she got. Vernon was breathing heavy and never wanting this moment to end, whispering to Sincere, "This is the best pussy I've ever had, it's so damn good please Sin I'm begging you don't ever take it from me, I don't know what I'd do, tell me it's mine."

The pleasure she was getting from Vernon at this moment had Sincere in a world of her own she would have told Vernon she'd jump over the moon. She kissed Vernon, looked at him with her green eyes very seductively, then said, "It's yours baby, this pussy is all yours."

Those words to Vernon were like saying, "Yes, Vernon I'll marry you.

He sexed Sincere all night. He couldn't stop. He felt like a dope fiend that had just had his first hit of crack. Sincere was his dope, and he had to have her. Sincere didn't know Vernon was thinking she was all his; she couldn't even be in another's man presence without him being there or saying it was ok.

Sincere is lying in Vernon's bed drifting off to sleep thinking she had to end this, she can't do this to Michael. Vernon lays beside her pulled her close to him thinking to himself, I'm never letting this woman out my life, this will be til death do us part, the old timer is out the box. He kissed Sincere's back, and then squeezed her tightly so she couldn't move; then they fell asleep.

Chapter 17

MICHAEL RETURNED

Waking up the next morning Sincere jumped out of Vernon's bed, took a shower then kissed Vernon, told him she'd call him later. Then rushed home to prepare for a business meeting she had with a contractor about making a patio for *Peaches N Cream.* As soon as she reached her bedroom, her cell phone rings, it was Michael, calling to let her know he's back and he wanted to see her soon as possible. He was on his way to her as they speak. Sincere was happy, but also surprised she wasn't expecting Michael until tomorrow night for their Valentine's Day date.

She let Michael know she's home and she'd be waiting for him. When Michael arrived with gifts for Sincere and the twins he said, he just couldn't leave New York without getting something that would bring a smile to her face!

Sincere gave Michael a kiss then guided him to her bedroom so they can have some privacy. She knew Michael would be expecting to have sex, she on the other hand was still sore from Vernon's twelve inch penis the night before. So she told him she wanted to wait for their special date tomorrow to have sex, but she had a treat for him.

She pushed him down on her California king bed, unzips his pants, pulled his penis out then began sucking it. Something she hadn't done to Vernon, but loved doing to Michael. Michael placing both his hands on her head told Sincere, she is the best; don't stop he loves the way her soft lips feel on him.

When he said, those words, it made Sincere take her hand and grip it on his penis, then move her hand up and down while she caresses the tip of his penis with her tongue. It drives Michael mad; he's making noises which make Sincere want to suck it even more. She took her hand, pushed his testicles up close and began putting her whole mouth on Michael's penis sucking it.

Then taking her tongue licking his testicles with her tongue Michael said, "Oh God what are you doing to me Sincere!"

Sincere not answering, just moving her mouth and tongue until finally she makes Michael cum. After he cums, Michael is laying on Sincere motionless thinking to himself, damn I have to marry this woman, and she's amazing in every way possible!"

Standing over Michael with a big smile because she knew she just gave him the best oral sex he's ever had. Sincere told Michael, don't move, then comes back with a warm soapy wash cloth, and began washing cum off Michael's body.

Michael laying there still motionless loves what Sincere is doing to him after a long week of business meetings, being stuck in crazy New York traffic. Coming home to this was just what he needed. He pulled Sincere down on the bed on top of him then started kissing her rubbing her big round ass he asked, "Baby can we just stay in your room all day and just hold each other. I don't want to move, I just want to lay here and hold you all day."

Sincere loving the idea, lifted her head up from Michael's chest then asked, "Do you want me in my birthday suit or in one of my sexy teddies?"

Michael bit his bottom lip then answered, "I want your sexy ass butt naked. A teddy will just cover up all this beauty you have. I want to look at every bit of you, if there's a pimple on your butt I want to see it, I love looking at you."

Sincere then took off her clothes pulled back the

covers and cuddled with Michael, pressed the intercom button to reach Annabelle downstairs then told her she wanted no interruptions. She is spending the day in bed. Annabelle let Sincere know she'd take care of everything, the twins and her home will be fine, get some rest.

However, she wasn't going to be resting, she was going to be enjoying Michael's company! Enjoying giving his penis attention all day. She put in her Donell Jones CD, plays no interruptions she thought to herself, yeah Michael was sure to be sprung by tomorrow morning."

Chapter 18

BY MY VALENTINE

HAPPY VALENTINE'S DAY baby, Sincere said, kissing Michael,, holding a tray with breakfast for the two of them.

Stretching and pulling the sheets over his waist, Michael grabbed the glass of orange juice off the tray then said, "Happy Valentine's Day baby this is the first of many! I hope what I have planned for you makes you the happiest woman in Georgia."

Sincere kissed Michael, told him to get up and eat his breakfast so he could see what she had gotten him. Michael sat up to eat the breakfast she had prepared. Sincere rushed him, stuffing food down his mouth.

Trying to take a bite and talk at the same time, Michael grabbed Sincere's hands and said, "Baby slow down you're putting food in my mouth faster than I can chew, obviously you want me to see my Valentine's Day gift. I can hold off on breakfast for a while, I have a couple of surprises for you as well."

He then got up, went into the bathroom to wash up, comes out headed straight down the stairs. Went out her front door to his car he popped the trunk then, pulled out a bag from *DONALD'S SAPPHIRE and DIAMONDS*, one of three biggest jewelry stores in downtown Atlanta. He hit his alarm then went back in the house, ran up the stairs to Sincere's room, where she's waiting with a sexy pink teddy on with white tights, and six inch pink stilettos with a big red bow wrapped around herself. She also was holding a bag from *DONALD'S SAPPHIRE and DIAMONDS.* He took one look at her and knew what he had in the bag had been no mistake; this is the woman he wanted to be with for the rest of his life.

He walked up to Sincere, softly nibbles her bottom lip then said, "I just want to eat your ass alive right now. You're so damn beautiful to me. I have to be the luckiest man in the world right now!"

Giving him a quick kiss on the lips, Sincere said, "You are, now come on, open your gift," placing the bag he had for Sincere on her bed. Michael then took the *DONALD SAPPHIRE and DIAMOND'S* bag from Sincere, smiling. She wanted to do this for him; it was a way of showing her love. She then took the watch and put it on Michael's wrist and said, "See its perfect, looks nice around your wrist," telling her he saw she had good taste in jewelry, taking the box out the bag.

She began to open the box; in it was a solid white gold watch with diamonds as the numbers. "Wow baby thanks, this is a very expensive watch you didn't have to do this; you spending time with me would of been gift enough," running her fingers thru his hair.

Michael now was even more anxious for Sincere to see what he had for her. He asked her to have a seat then took her hand and said, "Sincere baby everyday has been like Valentine's Day since I met you; not a day goes by that I don't want to feel your touch; every breath I take I think of you and I hope that you're thinking of me that way too! "Baby, I don't know what life is going to bring me in the future; however, I do know whatever life brings I want you standing there beside me. I love you Sincere Simmons. I want to spend the rest of my life with you!"

Michael then got down on one knee, pulled a small box out the bag, opened it showing the 10 carat diamond and said, "Sincere baby, will you make me the happiest man in the world baby, will you marry me?"

Sincere so choked up by the words he just said, hugs

Michael tightly with tears in her eyes she said, "Yes Michael! Yes, I will marry you and I would be honored to be Mrs. Michael Saint John."

Now engaged for the total of five minutes, Sincere is ecstatic she told Michael, "I have to tell my parents, oh my God, I'm getting married," rushing over to call her parents. Sincere grabbed the phone, but before she could get it off the receiver it rings, she answered so excited, "Hello!" It was Vernon, "*HAPPY VALENTINE'S DAY,* baby I miss you," covering the phone, Sincere looks over at Michael telling him it's an important call she'd have to step out the room for a minute. Then walked out the room to finish talking with Vernon, "Happy Valentine's Day Vernon honey, it's good to know I've been on your mind." "Of course you've been on my mind sweetness, you're all I've been able to think about lately; that's why I'm calling, you know it's Valentine's Day and I want us to spend the whole day together. I got something special for you, can you meet me at my house in a few hours?"

Sincere paused for a moment before saying "Aww, Vernon sweetheart there is nothing more I'd rather do than to spend Valentine's Day with you,; but I've already made plans prior to this for me plus the kids to join my parents and baby sister for dinner.

If you want I could still come visit you for a little while before I have dinner with my parents?" Vernon agreed to that and they hang up the phone. Walking back to her room Sincere can't believe she just lied to Vernon like that; however, she couldn't tell him she was going to dinner with Michael. He just had proposed to her, she knew Vernon wouldn't understand that because he too wanted a relationship with her. Sincere figures she'd break the news to Vernon when she meets him.

She had to get rid of Michael until it was time for them to go out to dinner. When she opened her room door

Michael was in the bathroom getting dressed, she kissed him, "Hey baby going somewhere?"

Placing his hands on her face then kissing her Michael said, "yes baby I am, I have to get things together for tonight. I want it to be special so I'll be picking you up around 10pm and make sure you bring that teddy," Michael gave Sincere a wink then he walked out the door.

Looking in her rearview mirror, glossing her lips before she got out her car to walk inside Vernon's home. Sincere is wondering how in the hell is she going to tell Vernon she is engaged to someone else. Putting her ring in her glove box, Sincere got out her car to go tell Vernon this heartbreaking news.

Vernon opened the door with a bright smile, "Hello baby you're looking beautiful, let me take your coat." Sincere hands Vernon her coat, then said to him she really needs to talk to him about something essential. Vernon kissed her and told her later, he got something to show her; he grabbed her hands, took her to his dining room where he had a beautiful candle lit lunch prepared, and sitting in a chair was a huge stuffed white teddy bear, that said, I'm yours the teddy bear was holding a small box. Vernon took the box, got face to face with Sincere whose heart is beating so fast, she's hoping Vernon is not going to do what she thought he was going to do.

Sincere grabbed Vernon's hands and began to say, "Vernon baby, it's something I want to," Vernon kissed her before she could even finish her sentence and he told her, shhh, I don't want you to say anything, just listen to me.

"Sincere baby, these last few weeks I've known you have been the best weeks in my life; you're all I think about, I want you. I need you."

"You're the only woman I want in my life, I know it's too soon to ask your hand in marriage, but," Vernon started to open the box he kissed Sincere again then finished what he was saying, "Baby I know it's too soon to ask you to be my wife so I'm just giving you my heart!" In the box were 5 carat heart shaped diamond earrings.

Sincere knew she loved Michael so she was hesitant to take the earrings from Vernon but he had already taken her earrings out, and placing the ones he bought in. Sincere felt so confused. She wanted to tell Vernon she's engaged but at the same time she didn't want to hurt Vernon because she liked him too. For different reasons it was more of a lust thing with Vernon; with Michael it was so much more than that. Vernon is kissing Sincere and she pulled away and told him he didn't let her give him his gift.

Then she reached in her purse, pulled out a big slip of yellow paper and told Vernon she went to *TERRY'S GAME HALL* and ordered him a pool table with everything to it. She also gave Vernon another slip of paper and told him someone should be delivering it soon, they might as well have lunch while they wait.

In the middle of lunch the doorbell rings. Vernon wiped his mouth, got up from the table to answer the door. Sincere followed behind him because she was excited to see Vernon face, when he saw it was the same pool table that he had told her he'd been wanting. When Vernon opened the door it was a big tall dark skinned black man with a clipboard in his hand; he looked at Vernon and said, "Yeah, you Mr. James? We're from *TERRY'S GAME HALL;* we're here to deliver your pool table." Vernon opened the door all the way so the men could bring his brand new pool table in, pointing to the basement stairs he told the men," You can take it right down there fellas."

He looked at Sincere and told her, "baby you really out did yourself, wow, I can't believe you got me the pool table I've been wanting!" He gave Sincere a big kiss; she smiled then told him it's the least she could do because she couldn't spend the whole day with him.

After the men set up the pool table, Vernon asked Sincere would she like to join him in a game before she had to meet her parents; he began setting up the pool table. When Sincere got something on her shoe and had bent down, Vernon caught a glimpse of her Sincere apple bottom, dropped the pool cue and pulled her pants down. He had ad his Valentine's Day chocolate and he didn't stop till he tasted the cream in the middle. To him Sincere had the milk chocolate that melts in your mouth and not in your hands and he wanted her melting all over his mouth.

Not having time for sex which Sincere was happy about, Vernon pulled Sincere’s pants back up and said, "You have to be on your way to meet your parents but I hope I gave you something to keep me on your mind." She gave him a kiss, let him know he did an amazing job, he's the best; that's why he's her sweet cookie then she headed home so she could shower and go to dinner with Michael.

Chapter 19

VEGAS BABY

Dressed in a red BC BG dress, her hair pulled up, Sincere walked down her stairs looking like a million bucks.

"Wow Cece you look dazzling, your date will be pleased," Ta'Miya said, holding Alexis in her arms, looking in a mirror in the hall fixing her earring.

Sincere gave Ta'Miya a big smile then said, "Aww thanks MyMy. I sure hope so."

Sincere and Ta'Miya had given each other nicknames. Sincere was called 'Cece' by Ta'Miya and Ta'Miya was called 'MyMy' by Sincere; both nicknames different from what other's called them.

Ding Dong the bell rings, "Oh my God, he's here and my makeup isn't right. MyMy will you be a dear, and get the door for me please, then tell my honey bunch I'll be right with him."

Holding baby Alexis Ta'Miya opened there to see Michael standing there holding three dozen white, red and pink roses looking at him in shock, Ta'Miya said, "Daddy your Cece's Mr. Right?"

Michael stepped inside Sincere's house then said, "Sweetheart my Sincere is the Cece you nanny for wow this is great I was nervous about you two meeting and you already know each other and speaking of my Sincere, where is she, I have a surprise for her?"

Walking out the bathroom making sure her hair was in place, Sincere saw Michael and Ta'Miya talking; she holds out her hands and said, "Aww baby, are those for me and I see you've met Ta'Miya my nanny."

Handing her the roses Michael laughed, "Know her, I raised her, she's my oldest daughter I've been telling you about."

Sincere holding the roses in her hand said, "Your daughter but her last name is Manahand not Saintjohn," TaMiya cuts in before Sincere can say anything else.

"Cece, I wanted to use my mom's maiden name so I can get ahead without feeling I accomplished something just because who my father is. I love who I am but I also want to make it in life without people knowing who my father is."

Happy to know she's known Michael's daughter the last few months. Sincere told Michael to have a sit in the family room while she put her roses in water then she'd be ready to go to dinner.

Clearing his throat before speaking Michael said, "Baby well that's the surprise I have for you we're not going to dinner we're flying to Vegas on a private jet. I booked us a three night stay at the *MGM HOTEL*. I figured it would be a perfect engagement getaway for the two of us."

Sincere sat the roses down and gave Michael a big kiss then said, "But baby, I'm not packed for three nights in Vegas, actually I'm not packed at all, let me run upstairs and grab a few things," Michael took Sincere by the arm then told her she doesn't have to worry about anything; she packed everything he needs when she put on that dress and they'll shop once they arrive in Vegas.

The two sit with Ta'Miya and the twins for a while before heading off to Vegas. Sincere is relieved that she already had a relationship with Michael's daughter, well at least one of them anyway, the other two lived with their mother in New York, however, Sincere was sure she'd get along just fine with them as well.

Before they get ready to go to the private jet, Sincere kissed her babies then tells Ta'Miya, Annabelle will be there to help her and she left all the numbers she'd need on the fridge. She'd be home in three days, thanks so much for keeping an eye on the twins.

Sincere is still kissing the twins finding it hard to leave them for three days while she's in Vegas when Michael said, "Baby come on they'll be ok, you can call them every five minutes if you want but right now I have a private jet waiting for us. I promise if anything went wrong we'll be out of Vegas faster than we got there."

Feeling a little more secure about them now, Sincere grabbed her clutch purse then she and Michael headed off to Vegas.

Looking out the window as the jet flies over Vegas, Sincere started rubbing Michael's arm saying, "Vegas looks so beautiful baby. I love you so much; you always make me feel so special. I'm going to make these next three days one's you'll never forget."

Entering their room at MGM Sincere and Michael don't waste any time taking each other's clothes off. Michael sat Sincere up on a table in their room then started kissing her from head to toe until Sincere stops him and said, "Wait baby, I have an idea, bring a chair then come out to the balcony with me."

Grabbing the chair from the table, Michael followed Sincere out to the balcony butt naked but asking, "Sin baby what if someone saw us?"

Sincere didn't care if anyone had seen them, in her mind there wasn't anyone else around only herself and Michael; she told Michael to sit down on the chair, then she straddled herself around him, kissing him softly; as she's kissing him she told him to squeeze her ass as Michael is squeezing Sincere is kissing his lips and neck passionately. She feels his penis getting hard and she was getting wet;

those two things were her cue to stick Michael's penis inside the softest place on earth. She took her hand then placed Michael penis inside her warm wet vagina then started riding him slowly.

Sincere is feeling so good to Michael, he's biting her neck, moaning loudly, "Oh sin baby, I love this pussy, ooooo baby, it's so damn good, and it's all mine, I love you," covering his mouth with her hands Sincere said in a low sexy voice, "Shut up and enjoy this ride."

After saying those words Sincere turned around with her ass in the air and started rubbing Michael's penis against her ass. She gently pushed it in then started riding Michael backwards with her ass muscles. That drove Michael delirious, he's moaning and shaking, begging Sincere to stop, but she loved having this control so instead of stopping she squeezed her ass cheeks tighter and grind even harder, and then kissed Michael at the same time, rolling his eyes in the back of his head.

All Michael could say, was thank you God, thank you Sin baby, please marry me, marry me tonight, hearing Michael say those words Sincere knew he would be wrapped around her finger and the next three nights in Vegas would be something to talk about but you know what they say *WHAT HAPPENS IN VEGAS STAYS IN VEGAS.*

Chapter 20

DID YOU FORGET ABOUT ME?

It's been four days since she's returned from her Vegas getaway and Sincere had been spending all her time with Michael and the kids. They were mending their pieces together to be a family because a date for the wedding was now set April 12, 2000 which was two years away, giving them enough time to see if this was really what they both wanted which they both were positive. Becoming Mr. and Mrs. Michael Saintjohn was what they wanted.

Having to come to the reality that she is not only a future mother and wife but she is the owner of two businesses that she had to run in her present. Sincere rushed to *House of Beauty* which she hasn't checked on since the day before Valentine's Day.

When she got in her office, she had a number of voice messages which makes her think she hadn't checked any of her voice messages from neither phone because she was dodging Vernon to spend quality time with Michael and the kids she realized she hadn't heard from Tyra nor Tavarious since Valentine's Day, that wasn't like neither of them not to try to contact her.

Pouring herself a cup of water, Sincere sat at her desk to begin listening to her messages, first message she heard is from Vernon, "Hey baby it's me. I've been calling your cell and haven't been able to reach you, so I'm leaving you this message on your office phone, give me a call. I'm worried."

Sincere is feeling bad inside because she did have a feeling of lust for Vernon, not love.

She hurry's and skips the rest of the message, the next

message she heard is from the muffled voice of Mr. Tony Anthony he said, and "Hello, this is Tony Anthony. this message is for Ms. Sincere Simmons, I'm looking forward to meeting with you next week here's the address where you are to meet me 2947 Flint Trace in *SLEDGE STONE CABIN ESTATES*, she smiled as she listens to the message and thought, "Hmm, I can't wait to meet this man that's willing to spend fifty grand for one night with me with no sex involved. Mr. Anthony you have me very interested in meeting you."

The next message she heard was Tyra "Hey Sin doll face it's me Tee, I've been blowing your cell phone up, where the hell you been, we can't get into the building, plus, I have some major tea for you with extra sugar with a dash of honey and your M.I.A. heffa call me when you get one of these messages. I'm at Tavarious new condo," hearing that message Sincere instantly picked up the phone on her desk and called Tyra; when Tyra answered she sounded happy and pissed at the same time, "Oh look who had arisen from the dead, good to know you're still breathing. The twins aren't walking are they?"

Laughing Sincere replied to Tyra, "Tee cut it out, I've been with Michael since Valentine's Day, he proposed then come to find out My is Michael's oldest daughter he's been telling me about and on top of all that Vernon thinks we're in a relationship, which I have sorta lead him on to think."

Tyra with her mouth open on the other end of the phone said, "Wow Sin girl shit I thought I had some tea with extra sugar with a dash of honey, girl you my make news sound like a welfare case," cutting Tyra off, Sincere said, "Yeah speaking of her tea girl what is it?" sounding very excited Tyra told Sin to come by Tavarious condo she's tell her then she gave her the address 1011 Kizzy Dale Ln in *ERLANDA MEADOWS CONDO'S* jotting down the address.

Sincere grabbed her Michael Kors purse to see what Tyra had to tell; she could hear the excitement in her voice. So Sincere knew this was going to be some really good news. She got to the Condo's and it's a huge maze of condos with so many different streets and every street name had a Dr. Ln. Circle, Ave. and Way.

Sincere shook her head and said to herself, "Tee, I'm going to get you for this one; this is some bullshit," driving for twenty minutes in this maze.

Sincere finally thought she'd made it to the right street; she looked up to see it said *KIZZY DALE CIRLCE,* not Kizzy Dale Ln frustrated, she picked up her phone, dialed Tyra's, cell when Tyra answered, Sincere said, "Look I've been driving in this confusing ass maze for almost thirty minutes now. I'm not driving in anymore circles. I'm parked in front of someone's condo on Kizzy Dale Ln and Glenda's Way you'll see my car. I'll be sitting here waiting for you to come find me."

Sincere then hung up the phone, turned up the radio to hear her favorite song the radio was playing, Nice and Slow by Usher, while she waited for Tee to meet her as she's poppin her fingers singing to the song her phone rings, it's Vernon, she turned down the music and answered, "Hey baby," Vernon surprised she answered but highly upset with her said, "Baby oh I'm baby now, Sin? I haven't heard from you in days you haven't returned any of my calls, I was worried sick; what have you been doing Sincere?"

With a frog in her throat almost scared to answer, Sincere said in a crackled voice, "Doing baby I haven't been doing anything. I actually was planning to come see you today, will you be home?"

Vernon said, uh huh be here by six, then hung up in Sincere's face. Sincere was kind of nervous about how that conversation just went. Sincere turned the music back up to now hear *Destiny's Child's, No No No,* trying to keep her mind off Vernon. She started singing the song by the time Beyoncé was starting the last chorus, Sin saw Tyra pulling up bobbing her head singing the same song, rolled down her window, looked at Tyra who's really into the song and said, "Come on girl let Beyoncé sing, you drive so I can follow you. I've been out here damn near an hour, your ass been in the house, let's move it lady!"

Tyra laughing, pulled her car right next to Sin's car and she rolled her window down, turned up the song even louder, started bobbing, snapping her fingers then said, "Wait Sin this my part Beyoncé young ass be blowing, this chick can sing," shaking her head laughing at Tee but bobbing her head hitting her hand to the beat on her steering wheel said, "Ooh Tee, you make me sick."

After the two ladies listen to the song, Sincere followed Tyra to Tavarious's condo. When they walk in, Paul and Tavarious are sitting on the couch playing Nintendo 64. Paul looked up and saw Sincere, he smiled holding his arms out saying, "Ahh shit Sin in the house, it's good to see you girl. Come around here and give me a hug girl, with yo sexy ass."

Walking over to hug Paul Sincere saw Kevin Millhouse coming out the bathroom out the corner of her eyes; her heart started to beat before she could say anything.

Tyra said, "Thanks for the gift Kevin, Tavarious and I appreciate it, you can leave now," giving a small chuckle Tavarious turned from playing the game and said, "Baby that was rude of you and Kevin just brought us a wedding gift," Kevin looked at Sincere then told Tavarious its okay; he was leaving anyway then walked out the condo's door.

Standing there wondering why Kevin was bringing a wedding gift over to Tyra and Tavarious and she had no idea there was even a wedding, Sincere gave Tyra a dirty look squinting her green eyes and lifting her eyebrow then said upset, "Umm, excuse me heffa, but did I miss something here; did I hear Kevin Millhouse say wedding gift and how the hell he knew about a marriage before me?"

Putting her hand on her hip giving Sincere the same look Tyra said, "Umm, excuse me Missy, I've been gone to Vegas with my future husband and haven't returned any of my calls for almost a week, if you would have answered your phone you would have known I found out I am four weeks pregnant and Tavarious was so happy we went got a marriage license and got married at the court house the next day no one was there, but us two. It was very simple. Perfect for me, because I never liked being in the spotlight," Sincere snatched Tee's hand off her hip, lifted her hand up to see her ring then said, "I'm pissed because I've always wanted to be your maid of honor at your wedding and plan a bridal shower you took that away from me however, I love the ring and I'm very happy for you congratulations Tee girl, I love you."

After hugging Tyra told Sin they can go into what was now her new bedroom, the two sat on Tyr'sa bed talking for hours like they did when they were younger which made Sincere lose track of time until her cell phone rings and she saw it's Vernon, she answered the phone to hear Vernon say, "I thought I asked you to be here by 6pm it's almost 7pm."

Sincere stuttering her words Sincere answered, "I know baby, I lost track of time sitting here talking with Tee. I'm on my way now promise."

When she hung up the phone Tyra said, "Aww Michael rushing you to spend more family time," putting her head down in shame.

Sincere answered, "No that was Vernon, and he wanted me to come over his house. So I am. I'll just catch up with you later babe alright."

Before Sincere can reach her bedroom door to get out, Tyra said, "Hey Sin wait, Vernon? U mean to tell me you're still talking to Vernon and you're wearing Michael's ring. You weren't raised to date two men at the same time and anyway I told you it's something about Vernon that scares me. But I'm backing off you're a grown woman. I'm going to let you handle your own grown woman situations."

Sincere gave Tyra a hug then assured her she had nothing to worry about, she can handle this. It wasn't nothing too serious just a sex thing with Vernon. It will die down soon. Then headed out the door speeding to Vernon's so she can make him happy since she'd been neglecting him lately.

When she pulled up to Vernon's she saw a dark blue Chevy Malibu parked in the drive way and a tall white man with a black hat and long trench coat on walking from Vernon's front door. She got out of her car and started walking to Vernon's door.

She passes, the man tips his hat then said, "Hello Ms. Simmons."

She said hello back, but was confused because she never met this man before. How did he know her name? She started wondering if he was a client of theirs. Sincere rings the doorbell, Vernon answered. He wasn't smiling this time, however, he kissed Sincere, told her come in he had dinner ready on the table, to have a seat because it's getting cold. Not wanting to upset Vernon, Sincere sits down quickly and started trying to have a conversation with Vernon who is being distant not saying much but staring at Sincere. While she eats he finally said, "Are you enjoying your meal baby?"

Taking a bite of her steak, Sincere smiled and said, "Yes."

Vernon rose from the table went in the kitchen then comes back with a big yellow envelope in his hand and placed it in front of Sincere. Chewing her steak she looked up at Vernon then asked,

"What's this?"

As she picked up the envelope to open it, Vernon didn't say anything he just stood over her. Sincere's eyes get so big when she saw what's in the envelope. In it were pictures taken by a private detective of her and Michael alone, then pictures of her Michael and the kids together. Sincere's heart started to beat so fast with fear because she knew Vernon was upset, she could see his eyes were red with anger, she tried to open her mouth to explain, but before she could Vernon had raised his hand and punched her so hard she had fallen out the chair onto the floor. She tried to get up, but Vernon punched her again making her fall back to the floor striking her a third time Vernon said to Sincere, "Bitch what did you think you were doing? Did you think I wouldn't find out you were giving my pussy away and that you were out parading around being the town whore? I'm about to beat the living hell out of you. You're mine! Do you hear me? So you better tell that nigga to get out your life, or I'm going to fuck him up too."

Shocked, shaking, and bleeding from what Vernon had just done, Sincere tried to get up from the floor to leave out of Vernon's home and never return. When she got on her feet Vernon pulled

her hair then asked, "Where the fuck do you think you're going? You're not going anywhere until I tell you, you can go."

Vernon then kicks Sincere in her stomach; she falls to her knees crying in pain. Vernon standing over her having no remorse for beating her said, "I love you, there isn't anything I wouldn't do for you, and to find out you're nothing but a beautiful whore, hurts me. You're nothing but a stuck up rich daddy's girl who thinks she can just do whatever she wants to people. Well do you know what I do to beautiful whores like yourself?"

Vernon puckers his lips then spits on Sincere. She

didn't fight back when he was striking her because deep down she felt she deserved it for playing with his feelings. However, spitting on

her had her so disgusted. She balls up her fist then punches Vernon right in his testicles, then ran out his door screaming for the next door neighbors to help her. She's looking behind her to see if Vernon was behind her as she is ringing Vernon's neighbor's bell furiously until a fourteen year old boy comes to the door. Sincere falls into the people's doorway saying, "Please can I use your phone to call the police? I've been beaten." The little boy saw Sincere bleeding badly, her right eye swollen shut, he started yelling, "Mom, Mom come quick, it's a lady hurt at the door. She's bleeding, mom call 911 quick!" The lady came running from the back of her home to see what her son was yelling about. Wiping her hands with a dish towel, she saw a bleeding Sincere on her floor, dropped her dishtowel then said, "Oh my God ma'am, what happened to you, Jerry honey call 911 this lady has been hurt."

Waiting for the police to get there, the woman of the house brought Sincere a wet cloth, then started wiping the blood from her face, never asking another question, just consoling Sincere until the police came.

When the police arrive at Vernon's neighbors home they see Sincere sitting in a chair beaten badly with her right eye swollen completely shut. The officer shines the flashlight on Sincere, then asked, "Ma'am who did this to you, and would you like to press charges?"

Looking up at the officer with one good eye Sincere answered, "Yes, I want to press charges. The man who did this name is Vernon James."

Chapter 21

MR. TONY ANTHONY

Sincere had been hiding out with her babies at a hotel in midtown Atlanta for three days not letting anyone know what happened or where she was, but Annabelle. The only reason she told

Annabelle was so she could bring her babies and some clothes to her.

Sitting on the hotel bed watching the twins sleep Sincere is bored thinking how is she going to still go on this date with Mr. Anthony when her eye wasn't healed yet. She couldn't cancel he had already paid the money and she had already spent a chunk of it investing in some things. So eye black or not Sincere knew she had to go on this date even after all that's happened. Tapping her perfectly manicured nails on the top of the hotel phone she decides to call Shay.

As soon as Shay answered Sincere can hear the loud music of Mystikal playing; she already knew what Shay was doing but she had to ask anyway, "Hey Shay toots, ya miss me? What are you doing?

Shay told Sincere to hold on. Turned down her music and got back on the phone then said, "What is it to do boo? I'm sittin here chillin, listening to my future husband Mystikal, smoking this blunt, with Paul's ass. But anyway, what u been up to cuz, yo ass been keeping a low profile these last few days bitch what's wrong, I know yo ass. What's the business? Talk to me. My ear listening, speak."

Sincere rolled her eyes in the back of her head, told Shay she thought she knew her. Then gave Shay the address to where she is and told her put the weed down, come talk to her, and then she hung up the phone.

Twenty minutes later Shay is knocking on Sincere's hotel room door.

Sincere opened the door asking, Shay to keep it down because the twins were still sleeping and she didn't want them awakened or she'd never be able to talk to her in peace, whispering, “Okay girl, we’ll need to go in that big ass bathroom to talk, because I want to know why you,” Seeing that Sincere had a black eye Shay went from wanting to know why Sincere been MIA to wanting to know who had blacken her eye and asked, "Um bitch what happened to yo eye, who dotted you in it?" Taking her hair moving towards her face to cover her eye Sincere answered Shay in a low voice of shame, "Vernon.” Shay hearing what she said, but wanting her to repeat it asked again, "Who did you say?" Sincere lifted her head up and said a little louder, "Vernon, Shay. I said, Vernon; did you hear me that time?"

Running her hand through her hair, blowing air out her mouth Shay said, "So Vernon a bitchass nigga, huh he put his hands on women. Sin I don't care what you say, I'm calling my cousin Tip over in Bankhead, he'll cut Vernon hand off and shove it down his throat. All I have to do is make a call.”

Holding her hands up, Sincere told Shay slow down, Vernon is in jail. She pressed charges so nobody had to cut nothing off anyone because he is in jail, and even when he's released he can't have contact with her.

Shay started turning up her lips telling Sincere, “Vernon lucky 5-O got him first because his ass was ou,.” then hurried to change the subject and asked laughing, "Okay Sin, so I know one of the reasons you called me out here is to let me see how Vernon kicked your ass, but what else is on ya mind?” I can tell it's something."

Looking into the bathroom mirror Sin turned around looking at Shay then said, "Ha ha ha very funny heffa, but you're right, I have to ask a favor of you."

Shay plops down on the toilet seat then asked, "What Sin? What is it, because this might be some bullshit like babysitting fucking wit yo ass.

Putting on make-up to cover up her black eye, Sincere gave a sly smirk and told Shay, "No, I don't want a sitter. However, I would like you to take the twins to Annabelle. Please stay in the hotel room until I return from a date. I have with this man named Tony Anthony. He paid fifty thousand dollars for one night with me, but no sex involved."

Shay let's Sincere know she thought it's something fishy about this Tony Anthony. Shay sat listening to Sin, but thinking, "What man pays fifty thousand for one night with a woman without at least smelling the pussy, without some bullshit being involved?" My girl beautiful and all, but I bet this nigga gon want some pussy by the end of the night." Shay got the twins ready to take to Annabelle while Sincere got ready to go on this fabulous date with Mr. Anthony. A date she had been looking forward to ever since she committed herself to it weeks ago. Pulling her royal blue Prada dress with her sterling silver custom made earrings and bracelets Lex had specially made for her as a Christmas present. No one in the world had a pair of earrings like them. Sincere loved those earrings more than she loved her money. Putting the earring in her ear, she glanced over at the clock and saw she was running late. Once again she hurry's up, pulled herself together and takes the thirty minute drive to *SLEDGE STONE CABIN ESTATES*. When she got there, she is very surprised to see how secluded it was. It was only a

few huge cabin homes, and they all were so far apart from each other you would have to drive to your nearest neighbor's home.

Looking trying to find *FLINT TRACE* Sincere is

thinking, "Lord where have I let this complete stranger lead me to."

Driving slowly, Sincere pulled up to a street and saw it said *FLINT TRACE.* She went down the long road leading to this big beautiful cabin home that looked as if it was just recently built.

She turned off her car, sighed, and then said to herself, "looked like Mr. Anthony just bought him a new home. Let me go in here and see what this man is all about and why did he specifically asked for a date with me, when I'm the owner not one of the workers."

Walking up to the door, Sincere saw it's a note taped on the door it said, "Hello Ms. Sincere

Simmons. I'm glad you came and I'm hoping to make this a night for you to remember. Please come in, the door is open and have a seat, I'll be right with you."

Thinking it was strange; Sincere opened the door and walked in. Mr. Anthony had it looking so beautiful. It was candles burning, soft music playing, and a bottle of Moet chillin in some ice.

Sincere is looking around wondering where is Mr. Anthony and why haven't he made an appearance yet. She walked over to his patio's double glass doors to peek and see if he was out there. No he wasn't there and there was still no sign of Mr. Anthony. Looking at the note again, Sincere decides to have a seat and wait for Mr. Anthony. She's giving him time just in case he's one of those men that like to make a very good first impression.

She's sitting in the chair with her eyes closed when she feels a man hands rubbing her shoulders and a strange feeling came over her body. It seemed to her as if she'd felt those hands before. Sincere still did not turn to look at Mr. Anthony. But she placed her hands on top of his while they sat on her shoulders.

Happy he finally got Sincere all alone Mr. Anthony said, "Hello Sincere, I'm so glad I can finally talk to you."

When Sincere heard Mr. Anthony's voice in person and it wasn't muffled like it was over the phone, it was clear she could hear it very well and it was a voice that she knew all too well. She turned around quickly to see Kevin Millhouse standing behind her.

Her heart dropped to her stomach, she began backing away before saying, "Kevin what are you doing? You're Tony Anthony?"

Kevin standing there with the look of pity on his face said, "Yes I am. I had to do something to get you to talk to me. Sin damn, I've been trying for years to apologize for what I did to you. I was wrong. I never should have taken something so special to you away so cruel."

Shaking nervously and still backing away from Kevin. Sincere still remembers he was the first man to ever hit her, and then he raped her. She took a deep breath and said, "Kevin you're forgiven. Forget about that night like I have and moved on. I'm going show myself the way out."

She started walking off. Kevin grabbed her roughly by her arm and told Sincere she's going to listen to him. Sincere not trying to hear Kevin's apology, snatched away from him. Sincere reached the counter where the bottle of Moet was chillin.

When Kevin grabbed her by her hair then said, "Sincere damn it you will listen to me bitch, I'm trying to apologize.

Having flashbacks of him raping her and Vernon just attacking her, Sincere grabbed the Moet bottle then hit Kevin in the head with it hard as she could. His head started bleeding severely and he falls to the floor. Sincere ran out the door frantic, jumping in her car speeding to the hotel where she knew Shay was waiting for her to return. When she got to the hotel, Sincere fixes her dress, put on a pair of her Prada shades and walked into the hotel. She headed straight to the elevator and to her room. When she opened the door Shay was laying across the bed watching TV.

Shaking, Sincere turned off the TV and said very franticly, "Oh my God Shay, Oh my God! Tony Anthony was Kevin Millhouse. He grabbed me, and then I hit him over the head with a bottle and ran." Shay hopping off the bed couldn't believe what she just heard. Asked Sincere to slow down and start over. She got up and gave her a bottle of water. Sincere began telling her what happened when she reached the so called Mr. Anthony's home, who was really Kevin Millhouse.

Pacing the hotel floor, Shay asked, Sincere, "So Sin is Kevin hurt or did you just get him really good."

With her head down and a million things running through her mind, Sincere answered, "I'm not sure Shay. I think I just got him really good, but he was bleeding so badly when I hit him with the bottle."

Shay told Sincere they have to go back to *SLEDGE STONE CABIN ESTATES* to at least see if Kevin had called the police on her. If they see the cops when they pull up, they'll know she'd have a case unless he don't tell it was her that busted his head.

Too nervous to drive, Sincere told Shay she had to drive, she can't even function. Shay took the keys and drives them to where Sincere left Kevin bleeding.

They pull up to Kevin's house, they see no police. Shay looked at Sincere and said, "See girl you worried for nothing, that nigga probably in there putting peroxide on that little cut right now. Even though we haven't fucked with Kevin since raping you, we still should go inside and make sure he did get the bleeding to stop."

Sincere still wiping tears from her eyes, a nervous wreck to go in took Shay's hand and the two enter Kevin's house together, walking in Shay is yelling, "Kevin it's me,

Shay. I'm here to check on ya nigga where you at."

Tiptoeing behind Shay, Sincere whispered, "Shay he fell in the kitchen."

The ladies walk to the kitchen to find Kevin lying on the floor bleeding from his head. Sincere ran to the kitchen sink to vomit, as Shay walked closer to Kevin who wasn't moving or breathing. She checks for a pulse to find out he doesn't have one. Shay's heart started to beat fast, as she slowly walked to the kitchen sink where Sincere was still sick.

Shay placed her hand on Sincere's back, "Get it all out honey; get it all out."

Once Shay had Sincere calm, she looked at her then asked, "Sin girl what the fuck happened here, you must have hit Kevin awfully hard with that bottle."

Sincere looked up at Shay to see a look of worry on her face which she had never seen before. She's never seen Shay have a worried moment since they met.

She asked, 'Shay Why? Why do you ask? Shay is Kevin hurt badly?"

Shay looked at Sincere not saying a word just holding her. Sincere knew then something bad had happened. She pulled away from Shay then went to the part of the kitchen where Kevin was lying to see he wasn't breathing.

Sincere knees got weak, she started crying, "Oh my God Shay! What have I done! He's dead! Oh no, I've killed Kevin Millhouse. I didn't mean to, I just wanted to get away from him, that's all. But he pulled my hair and I got so scared I just grabbed the bottle to hit him with. Oh God, I'm going to jail. I won't see my babies grow up, and then when I die I'm sure I'm going to hell for this one Shay."

Knowing she had to be the one to think fast because Sincere was in no position to think. Shay shook Sincere and told her snap out of it. They have to clean up the house from top to bottom leaving no sign of evidence that they were ever there.

Putting her arm around Sincere she said, "Stop crying now Sin this is no time to cry, you're leaving your DNA everywhere, besides if you go to hell you know I'll be there to pick you up."

Making Sincere look in her eyes, Shay keeps repeating to Sincere, "You didn't do this do you hear me, you didn't do this, you stick to that and you'll be fine. You know I have your back through thick and thin. You will see Alex and Alexis grow up, just remember what I told you. You didn't do this!"

The ladies clean all the evidence from Kevin's home, not leaving anything to trace back to Sincere. The police wouldn't know what happened.

Shay looked around and saw that everything looked perfect, and then shook her head and said, "Uh uh, this shit looked too perfect."

She went to the wine rack got a bottle of Moet then breaks the bottle, so she and Sincere can leave never returning there again and never, never mentioning what had happened in Kevin Millhouse's home.

The two ladies drive to Sincere's house. Sincere got out of the car and went into her bedroom. She locks the door, lays in the bed crying herself to sleep, wishing what had happened was just another one of her terrible nightmares.

Chapter 22

WHO MURDERED KEVIN MILLHOUSE

It had been a week and no one had said anything about finding Kevin Millhouse dead. Sincere had been a nervous wreck not being able to sleep nor eat while Shay went on like she didn't have a care in the world. However, she had been staying with Sincere to make sure she didn't break and go to turn herself in to the police, confessing to a murder they obviously knew nothing about yet.

Sincere is changing Alexis in the family room when the doorbell rings. She yelled for Shay to answer it. When Shay opened the door, Tyra busts through the door with Tavarious behind her crying. Tyra said, "Girl quick turn to Channel 2 News. Where's Sin she gotta see this!"

Tyra running towards the family room to turn on the TV. Sincere is on the floor, now changing Alex, looked at Tyra flying through her family room looking for the remote.

Sincere looking confused said, "Tee slow down girl, why are you looking for the remote which one of your TV shows are you missing."

Tyra finds the remote then said, "No Sin this isn't one of my TV shows doll face. How I wish it was. You must have heard it's been on all the local news stations. Kevin Millhouse was found dead this morning in a home no one knew he had."

Sincere stops in the middle of changing her sons diaper to look at Tavarious crying. Then she gave Shay that look like what had she done, sitting there in the state of shock.

Sincere's mind went blank until she heard Tyra said,

"Okay, okay, here it is, they're showing it again." Tyra turned up the TV so everyone could hear what the news was saying, "Today the body of 26 year old Kevin Millhouse was found in a home on *FLINT TRACE in SLEDGE STONE CABIN ESTATES*. There are no leads in the case as of yet, however, police are at the crime scene looking for clues and is asking if anyone knew anything about this homicide please contact the Atlanta Police Department. They want to give closure to Mr. Millhouse's family.

With a frog in her throat Sincere asked Tavarious, "So Tavarious they don't know who would want to do this to Kevin. How was Kevin murdered, and when?"

Trying to hold himself together to answer Sincere's questions, Tavarious wiped his eyes with his hand then responds, "Right now the police have nothing. Kevin had just closed on that house two weeks ago; no one even knew he had purchased it. I don't understand how something like this could happen who would want to kill Kevin. The police said, he was struck in the head with a bottle that cut a main artery which caused him to bleed out. Man this got me so messed up right now."

The four of them sit in Sincere's family room for hours talking about their childhood years with the Millhouse boys and who would want Kevin Millhouse dead. Shay returned from the kitchen took a seat back on the sofa stuffing chips in her mouth looking sweet and innocent said to the others.

"Well guys, it's sad and all what happened to Kevin, but real talk, we don't know what Kevin was into or who he had done something to. It's a fucked up world and unfortunately folks only let you know what they want you to know about their personal lives."

Agreeing with her, Tyra took a few chips out the bag, looked at Tavarious, who's taking Kevin Millhouses death quite hard, then said, "ladies sorry to bring you such awful news today, however, it was good seeing you two spending time with ya it's been real, but now I have to get my husband home and help him ease his mind. He's hurting right now," Tyra grabbed her purse from Sincere's table and rubbed Tavarious shoulders. Then the newlyweds leave Sincere's house.

Watching the 11:00 o'clock news, Sincere and Shay saw the police still had no leads on the Kevin Millhouse murder even though they both knew what happened to Kevin.

Neither would ever speak a mumbling word about it and Sincere always repeated in her head what Shay told her, "I didn't do it; I did not kill Kevin Millhouse."

Looking over at Shay enjoying playing with the twins, Sincere asked Shay if she minds staying up with the twins while she went to bed. When she reached her bedroom, Sincere lays there crying wishing she could turn back time and take back what happened that night in *SLEDGE STONE CABIN ESTATES*. She asked God to forgive her for what she had done, buried her face in her pillow and cried all night long.

Chapter 23

WHEN IT RAINS IT POURS

It's a cold rainy Saturday morning and also the day that Kevin Millhouse would be laid to rest. Sincere had been debating all morning if she should attend the funeral. She feels so bad about killing Kevin she didn't want to attend his funeral, however, the police was still investigating and she didn't want to give them any reason to ask her anything. So she pulled a black dress out her closet then called Shay.

Shay lets the phone ring several times before answering, "Yeah, state ya bizz."

Sincere smacks her lips and said, "Really Shay must you answer the phone like that, can you be a lady sometimes besides when you have a dick stuck off in you," laughing loudly.

Shay answered, "Hell naw you know I can't, I'm Shay aka gangsta boo, this what I do booboo."

Changing the subject, Sincere asked Shay was she going to Kevin Millhouse's funeral. She thought it would be best if they attended his funeral like all the other people in the neighborhood. It wouldn't be a good look if they weren't there. Shay lets Sincere know she'd be going and she would be riding with her. She'd be at her house in an hour.

When Shay arrived at Sincere's, it was twenty minutes before the funeral started.

Sincere comes running out the house before Shay can even get out her driver's seat saying, "Girl you might as well drive. Your car is already on and you got ya seat belt on. Let's go pay our respects to Kevin. We might as well, because I'm already going to hell for this."

Pulling off, Shay looked at Sincere and said, "Bitch would you please stop saying you're going to hell for something you didn't do. Plus I keep telling you Sin if you go to hell I'll be there to pick you up, you just sit there until I get there."

Pulling into *THE HOUSE ON A HILL CHURCH*, the ladies see the funeral line proceeding to go into the church, Sincere's heart started beating hard and her hands begin to shake.

She pulled on Shay's coat sleeve then whispered, "Shay I don't think I can do this. I'm a nervous wreck. This can't be right attending this funeral," Shay pinches Sincere on her arm hard and said smiling but not moving her lips, "Sin cut it out right now! It's too late, we're here now, shut the fuck up before you blow your cover damn." Walking up to the church doors, Sincere's knees got weak and she started telling herself, "I can do this, I don't have to look at Kevin in his casket. I can walk right passed him and have a seat."

Getting closer to Kevin's casket, all you could hear is his mother, Mrs. Millhouse crying. It was a cry that came deep from the heart, "Oooooohhh, awwwww, my baby, ooooooooooh Kevin baby. God gonna take care of you for me nowwwww."

Sincere hearing his mom cry in such pain began to cry because she too was a mother, and she couldn't imagine ever having to bury one of her children. The fact this lady was mourning the death of her son was all because of her broken her heart.

"Come on," Shay said, pulling Sincere's arm because they were next to view Kevin's body.

"I can't do this Shay," Sincere said, pulling Shay's arm back, and Shay pulled Sincere up to view the body of Kevin Millhouse. When Sincere looked at him, tears ran down her face. She was having flashbacks of when they were sitting in the chair laughing, the rape, their argument at her eighteenth birthday party, and of course, the night of the murder.

"Sin Sin baby, come on, it's alright," Shay said, hugging a devastated Sincere from Kevin's casket.

They took a seat next to Donaven and Vincent Hightower's, two twin brothers they went to school with. Donaven was 5'9, small afro nicely groomed, a mocha colored man, and his brother Vincent was the opposite. He was 6'2, nice fade, no facial hair, and he had nice carmel skin, both men very attractive.

"Hey Sin, nice seeing you not under these circumstances, but it's real good seeing you, looking good girl." Vincent Hightower whispered to Sincere when she scooted next to him on the church pew.

"Thanks Vince you're looking real good yourself baby," Sincere said, winking at Vince.

Many people didn't know this, but Vincent and Sincere had history together. He used to have a huge crush on Sincere. Their lockers were next to each other all of high school and every day at school he would leave a rose and a note that said, "someone thinks the world of you, bet cha can't guess who."

"We all have to go this very same way; every man had a time to be born and a time to die. Kevin's time here on earth had now passed, his journey to eternity had begun," said Pastor Jerry White, to a church full of people.

HOUSE ON THE HILL CHURCH was a very small church, people were sitting arm to arm, barely lifting their arms to wipe the tears from their faces, but it was Mrs. Millhouse's church home of 25 years, so she wouldn't have it no other way.

Shay is sitting in the church thinking to herself,

"Thank God Sincere Bath and Body Works, works cause I hate strange smells like the funny smell coming from the lady that just sat next to Sin and Vince man. It's packed in here like a can of sardines and it's hotter than cow balls. Gosh, so not the time for this lady not to have bathed; she came to pay her respects but didn't respect herself enough to wash her butt, wow the things you see at funerals."

Sincere unlike Shay was saddened by this and focusing on what Pastor Jerry White was saying, she was thinking, "Man this man can really preach. I feel like he is talking to my soul. I needed to be here listening to the word," Sincere took a deep breath then got a whiff of the strange smell, Shay was thinking, making a funny face, then said to herself," Oh my, what is that God awful smell and I know it's not me nor Shay. It had to be this beautifully made up woman with this nice Chanel dress on. Hmm, she was worrying about her looks but not smell. Geez, who does that, Whew, I just hope no one thought it was me?"

Coming out of the church everyone is visiting before they meet up at the cemetery to lay Kevin Millhouse completely to rest.

"Sin, are you going to the burial sweetheart?" Vincent Hightower said, following her to her car. "Naw, I'm going to pass on the burial and repass. I have to get home to my babies," Vincent stepped back, looked Sincere up and down, giving a big smile then said, "Baby girl, you don't look like you have any kids. Congratulations on the babies and on keeping all that together."

Sincere gave Vince a flirty laugh, nudged him and said playfully, "Aww, Vincent stop it boy, you're too much. But thanks babe, I sure do try to keep it all intact.

Looking at her licking her lips, Vincent said, "Naw baby you ain't gotta try, you're doing it and doing it well. I must say."

Vincent and Sincere exchanged numbers, give hugs,

and make plans to get together for a friendly dinner. Then Sincere and Shay head to Sincere's house to start planning the surprise bridal shower for Tyra, even though she's already married. Sincere wanted to do something special for Tyra; she was like a sister to her. She feels she wasn't a part of her special day, but she would give Tyra another special day that she and all their friends could be a part of.

Finally reaching Sincere's house, she and Shay began jotting down everything they needed and who to invite to Tyra's shower. After hours of writing, making phone called, and snacking, Sincere and Shay had planned out the perfect bridal shower.

The hardest thing for Sincere was not telling Tyra about what she's planning. Tyra and Sincere are like chitterlings and hot sauce, without each other it's just not right so keeping this from Tyra is a challenge for Sincere. She cannot wait to see the look on her face. She did it! The bridal shower was a success.

It's been months since Kevin Millhouse had been buried. There were still no leads, and his case was growing cold which left injustice for his family. Sincere calmly stayed focused on what mattered most, her children and her future husband, Michael.

Waiting for Michael and Ta'Miya to return from the video store they could have a family movie night with movie, popcorn and pizza.

Looking over in their playpens, Sincere noticed the twins were napping, so she decided she was going to take this time to relax and read a book, something she hadn't had time to do in a while.

Sincere sits the book down, looked out the window and said to herself, "Ooh, it's raining out now, well that cancels me and the twins walk to the park."

She went and checked to see if Alex and Alexis were still sleeping. They were, so she went into the kitchen to fix her a sandwich. While preparing her sandwich, the phone rings, it was her father, Sammy. He was calling to tell her she and the twins were going to dinner with them tonight, so be ready by 7pm. After speaking with her father, Sincere went to the family room, picked up the remote then flicked through the channels.

While she ate her sandwich the doorbell rang. She let out a sigh, sat her plate on her table then headed to the door without looking thru the peep hole or asking who it was.

Sincere flung her front door open to see the police standing there; the officer looked at Sincere's handcuffs, and said, "Sincere Simmons, you're being charged with the murder of Kevin Millhouse."

Alexis lets out a loud cry, Sincere jumped, her book falls to the floor, she wiped her face and eyes with her hand, looked around with her heart beating out her chest then said, "Whew oh my God, it was just a dream another fucked up dream. I swear this shit had got to stop Picking up Alexis, Sincere saw her diaper had failed her in her sleep. Poor little princess had pee all over her and that's why she was crying so loudly. She wanted that nasty urine off of her, "Awwww momma's princess, your pamper just gave up on ya, huh, let momma give you a bath so you can be my princess again, smelling like baby magic and not the Citgo gas station up the road."

After bathing Alexis, Sincere played with her beautiful baby girl, thanking God for blessing her with such beautiful healthy children.

She kissed Alexis's chubby cheeks and said, "Baby girl if your daddy could see what a precious diamond we made he would be so thrilled, you wouldn't be able to have a social life, but he would have been a proud father."

RING RING, both Sincere's cell and house phones rang, waking up baby Alex. Sincere was trying to pick up her crying child and figure out which phone to answer. She picked up her house phone to hear her mom Neicy yelling something in her ear, but she couldn't make out what it was her mom was saying. So she told her mom, hold on, she couldn't understand her.

She had MiMi call her cell. Sincere answered her cell, "Hello MiMi."

MiMi sounded very upset on the other end. She told Sincere her father had collapsed and had been rushed to Golden Heart Hospital. Sincere hung up the phone, grabbed her babies and called Michael.

She told him, "Something had happened to her father and to meet her at Golden Heart Hospital."

Minutes felt like hours to Sincere as she's speeding to see what had happened to her father. With tears in her eyes, she prays to God for him to keep her father here on earth; they have so many more memories to make. She started apologizing for what she did to Kevin, asking God, please don't take her father for what she had done, and take her.

Sincere is pulling into the hospital parking lot waiting for Michael who is getting out his car so he can get one of the twins. When Michael got to the car, he gave Sincere a big hug and kiss, then, got baby Alex out of his car seat.

Sincere got Alexis, then looked at Michael and asked, "Baby do you believe in Karma? I sure do and when it rains it pours."

Chapter 24

SAMMY'S BIG BATTLE

It had been a month since Sincere and her family found out her father, Sammy, was battling cancer; a battle he had been fighting alone the last eight years. He didn't want Neicy or his girls worrying. He was just making all the necessary arrangements that were needed for his funeral and his family being taken care of fully financially, when he was gone.

Sincere is holding Alex in her lap, as she is sitting in the chair next to her father's bed. He's been home from the hospital a week now and Sincere hadn't left her father's side. Rubbing his hands as he rested, she's thinking how could a man so strong, so powerful, handsome, outgoing and full of life now be so weak and fighting to survive each day.

She wanted this to be a dream she'd soon be waking up from. But with each passing day she was realizing it was reality. She was losing her father and all the money they had wouldn't make a difference. It was nothing they could do. The Lord's will had to be done, it had to be done. However, Neicy and Sincere prayed every day that Sammy would get better, fight a little longer. He had to walk Sincere down the aisle on April 12, 2000 and it was currently October 15, 1998, three days before the twins first birthday.

Neicy was planning her grandbabies a huge first birthday party at their home. So Sammy wouldn't have to go far, just in case he felt ill during the twins birthday party hours. Neicy was so excited, as she called to confirm the carnival rides and the circus act for Alex and Alexis. Sincere had no idea what a big bash her babies were having for their first year on earth.

Glancing through her party to do list for her grandbabies, Neicy is thinking about how a year ago Sammy asked her could they try for a son. He knew they were getting old, but there was nothing more he wanted than for Neicy to give him a son to play football with, take fishing and do all the father and son things. Sammy loved his girls, pony rides, having tea parties, watching them play dress up, but he always wanted a son to teach him to be a real man, and a provider for his family.

A tear falls from Neicy’s eyes because she wishes now she could try for a son, but with Sammy going to his chemo treatments every six weeks. She didn't think he was strong enough to have sex to even make a baby. Sincere walked in, seeing her mom with a pen and pad. She peeks over her mom’s shoulder, trying to see what she was writing.

Then said, "Hey mom, what cha writing down?

Things daddy needs done, I can help if you need me to. I have nothing else to do, except focus on daddy. I haven't even had time to plan my children a first birthday, which is awful of me."

Neicy pats Sincere on the shoulder and told her don't worry about her father, he'll be alright, she’d take care of him then told Sincere she was going to buy the twins a cake and they could have a very small birthday party with just them on Saturday.

Sincere gave her mom a hug then thanked her for being such a wonderful mother and wife. She appreciated her, and then she headed back upstairs to attend to her father. Sincere hated being away from him, she wanted to make every day he had left special in every way, even the simplest things.

Like watching her father brush his teeth brought her joy, knowing her father woke up to accomplish that one more day was a heartfelt feeling. Sincere could sit with her father every day without having a dull moment.

Its Saturday October 17th, 1998, the day before Alex and Alexis turned 1, and the day of the big surprise party Neicy was giving them. Sincere wakes up in the chair next to her father, it had been her bed since Sammy came home from the hospital. She couldn't sleep at night unless she was near him.

She stretches, then kissed her sleeping father on the forehead and walked out the room so she could check on Alex and Alexis. When she reached the spare room, they'd been sleeping in; she saw her babies were not there. She headed downstairs. Walking toward the kitchen she heard laughing and smells breakfast cooking. She walked in the kitchen, Michael was talking with her mother and playing with Alex.

Sincere kissed him then said, "Good morning baby, Good morning momma."

Walking over to the fridge for a glass of orange juice she stops by the stove first where MiMi is cooking. Sincere grabbed a slice of bacon and let's MiMi know the breakfast smells wonderful. She then pours a glass of OJ and sat at her parent's kitchen table with Michael and Neicy.

Took a sip of juice, looked at her mother and said, "So mother, what time are you getting the cake today? I want to know what time to have the twins ready. Even though it's just us, I still want them looking fabu, like their momma."

Neicy looked at Michael giving him the cue to cut in.

Michael clears his throat before saying, "Hey baby, that's why I'm here so early, I wanted to take you and the kids to this new place that just opened, *LIZZY'S BOTANICAL GARDEN and AQUARIUM.* I thought it would be a nice family outing for Alex and Alexis's first birthday. Since we'll already be out, we'll stop and pick up the cake for your mother."

Sincere got up from the table, gave Michael a long kiss then said, "Aww baby, you always have the perfect ideas. God had sent me the perfect man."

Taking Alexis out of Neicy's arms, and then telling Michael to follow her with Alex. Sincere went up her parent's stairs to her old bedroom so she and Michael can get the twins ready for the family outing. After they're all dressed for a day of family fun, Sincere put on the twins jackets and asked Michael can he handle getting them to the car while she grabbed their diaper bags.

Michael being the gentlemen he is, took the twins and both diaper bags, and then told Sincere to meet them in the car, they'll be waiting. Sincere put on her jacket, grabbed her LV purse then started down the hall to her father's room where she thought Sammy would be sleeping, but when she got in her father's room he was sitting up, eyes wide open, watching THE JEFFERSON'S laughing. Sammy used to love watching it when Sincere was a kid.

Giving him a big smile Sincere walked in saying, "Hey daddy, I see you're feeling good today. I'm happy to see that."

Sammy looked up from the TV, gave Sincere a hug and a kiss on her forehead then said, "Yeah baby girl, I feel wonderful today. I'm going to get dressed so I can join my family to help celebrate my grandbabies first birthday. Ya know I don't know how many more I'll be able to see them celebrate."

Sincere rubbed her hand over her dad's head then said, "Oh daddy, don't talk like that, you're going to beat this thing. You're going to live forever."

Giving her father a kiss on the forehead, Sincere told him she was leaving for a few hours, she'd be back around 4pm so they could have cake and ice cream for the twins.

Sincere is rushing to the car with her purse hanging from her shoulder when she hopped in the car.

Michael smiled at her then said, "Oh you are joining me and the twins. We were about to leave you baby."

Laughing Sincere said, I would have jumped in my car so fast; I would have been at *LIZZY'S BOTANICAL GARDEN and AQUARIUM* entrance when y'all pulled up. Leaving me, not happening, Captain you and the twins stuck for life." Sincere then holds her left hand showing off her 10ct diamond ring.

When they get to *LIZZY'S BOTANICAL GARDEN and AQUARIUM* , it was beautiful; a huge glass building with an indoor garden with one of the largest aquariums attached to it. Sincere fell in love when they entered the inside.

She looked at Michael and told him this is where she wanted to hold her wedding ceremony and reception. It would be perfect for their special day; besides, it would be different, no one would think to get married at an aquarium.

They're watching the dolphins swim when Ta'Miya comes behind Sincere poking the sides of her stomach then said, "Boo," jumping.

Sincere turned around to see it was Ta'Miya. She laughed and told Ta'Miya she almost gave her a heart attack, then asked why she was late getting there, it was time for them to be leaving now.

Looking at her father, Ta'Miya told Sincere she had to make a few stops before joining them and then she got caught in traffic.

Michael looked at his watch and let's Sincere know they have to be leaving if they wanted to make it to the bakery to pick up the cake for her mother. When they pulled up to the bakery, Sincere saw how nice the sign *PUNKIN'S CAKES and PIE'S* looked. It was decorated with cute little pumpkins and different types of desserts.

She walked into a sweet lady with a bright smile, her name tag said, Mo'nique. She said, "Hello, welcome to *PUNKIN'S CAKES and PIE'S.*

Are you here picking up an order, or you're just looking for something to satisfy your sweettooth?"

Sincere gave her a nice smile, and then told her she was there to pick up an order for Neicy Simmons. Mo'nique then went to the back and comes out with this huge birthday cake. Sincere makes a confusing face, telling Mo'nique there must be some mistake. Her mother ordered a small birthday for her twins first birthday.

Mo'nique looked at the order form looked back at Sincere then said, "Nope ma'am there's no mistake. Mrs. Neicy Simmons ordered this cake. She even brought in a photo and had us put it on the cake."

Sincere peeks over the counter to see the huge cake with Alex and Alexi's picture on that said, "HAPPY 1ST BIRTHDAY ALEX and ALEXIS YOU HAVE BROUGHT SO MUCH JOY IN OUR LIVES."

Sincere shook her head, looked at Michael then said, "Oh my gosh my mom is so over the top, we're going to be eating birthday cake for Thanksgiving at this rate and where does she expect us to put this huge cake. Ugh that lady can stress me out sometimes even though her thought was kind.

Michael told Sincere don't worry about the cake, hands her his credit card to pay for the cake and told her he's going outside to make room for the cake.

When Michael walked out the bakery Sincere looked at Mo'nique behind the counter then said, "Girl he's going to stress me too trying to squeeze this cake in the car with us."

Mo'nique giggled then said,"Well here's some of our famous turtle cookies, you know what they say, stressed is desserts spelled backwards, eat one of these cookies,"

Sincere took the bag of cookies given to her.

Sincere said, "Thanks Mo'nique.

When she got outside, there is a small delivery truck parked in back of them and Michael was speaking with the driver.

He looked over at Sincere saying, "Baby he's going to deliver the cake to your parents' home so you don't have to be stressed."

Sincere gave him a kiss and told him he's the best, always putting her needs and wants first, she couldn't have asked for a better man.

"What have my mom done! I knew she had something up her sleeve when I saw that cake and you knew about this too Michael," Sincere said, as they pull in her parents drive to see cars everywhere?

A big birthday banner with the twins faces on it said, happy birthday, the circus act and carnival rides covering her parent's backyard.

Michael kissed Sincere then said, "Yeah baby I knew all about it. Your mother and Mrs. Foster planned it and asked me will I take you guys out while they set up everything."

HAPPY BIRTHDAY ALEX and ALEXIS, everyone yelled when Sincere and Michael walk in with the twins. Everyone and all of Lex's family and friends and all of the Simmons family, of course was there showering the twins with many gifts and love. Sincere is enjoying her baby's first birthday party, but part of her is sad because Lex wasn't there to share this moment.

She didn't know how many more birthdays or other holidays her father would have with them, however, she became happy when she saw her pregnant cousin Tyra waddling towards her. Tyra was due on Halloween and big as ever. She didn't want to know what she was having as long as it was healthy she would be happy.

"Hey big momma," Sincere said, rubbing Tyra's belly.

"What's up Sin? I'm so ready to have this baby. I want my body back. I breathe like a bull, I'm never getting pregnant again I swear, I'm getting my tubes tied."

Sincere laughed at Tyra, and then told her, "Tubes come untied, don't let anyone fool you. If God saw fit, you will be blessed with more than one child. Tubes tied or not, honey. So just be fruitful and multiply like the bible said."

They're sitting at the table eating while Tyra is telling Sincere the baby names they've picked out, while she's feeding the twins.

"We like Jeremiah Ja'Zerre Campbell, if it's a boy and Rachel Annette Campbell, if it's a girl."

Sincere let Tyra know she loved the names they have chosen for her new bundle of joy. Tyra stands up to go to the bathroom then felt a sharp pain. She told Sincere, "she doesn't know what a contraction feels like but she's pretty sure she just had one."

When she comes from the bathroom she wanted her to time them if she had anymore. Sincere let's Tyra know she'd be out there waiting, feeding the twins.

By the time Tyra finally comes out the bathroom everyone had finished singing happy birthday to the twins and Sincere was cutting their cake.

She looked up, saw Tyra was out the bathroom and said, "Hey hun how ya feeling?" Tyra rubbed her belly then told Sincere.

I'm fine, if I can just stop peeing. That's why I stayed in the bathroom, because soon as I would finish, zip up, and wash my hands, I'd have to pee again.

They both laugh, but when Tyra laughed, she felt a gush. She looked nervously at Sincere and said, "Sin I believe my water just broke, because I know I didn't just pee on myself."

Excited, Sincere got up from the table and announces to everyone, "Everybody I need your attention. I want to thank everyone for coming out showing me and my children love, however, Tee's water just broke and I am going to the hospital with her and Tavarious. You are all welcome to stay and enjoy the food, carnival rides, and the circus animals, but I have a baby to see being brought in this world."

Neicy told Sincere, she and Michael can go to the hospital with Tyra, but the twins were staying at their first birthday party with them and their guests.

Pulling up to *GLENDA'S LIFETOUCH HOSPITAL*, Sincere is running in the double doors to catch Tyra and Tavarious because Tavarious was pushing Tyra so fast in the wheelchair, you would have thought they were in a race.

In the labor and delivery room, Tyra is screaming to the top of her lungs, she can't take pain at all. When she's on her period, it had her down for three days. So the contractions felt like she was dying with each one.

Sincere leaned over her, placing a cold towel on her forehead then said, "Tee you have to stop screaming. With the contractions blow, just blow the pain away. If you yell it's making it worse. Breathe baby, just breath."

Sincere then told Tavarious he needs to comfort his wife. Tavarious was very nervous, pacing the delivery room floor not knowing what to say, not wanting to touch Tyra, because he didn't want to upset her while she was in so much pain.

After being in strong labor for only six hours Tyra gave birth to a healthy beautiful baby girl. She was now a mommy. A warm feeling of love came over her. Once Tyra held her new baby girl; she knew she could never love anyone as much as she loved this child she just brought into this world. Sincere was crying, congratulating Tyra and

Tavarious for becoming new parents. Then she took her camera out her purse and began taking pictures of the new addition to the Campbell family.

Kissing Tyra's baby girl before snapping a picture, Sincere said, "Welcome to the world Rachael Annette Campbell."

It's been over a year now that Sammy had been fighting his battle with cancer. The doctors had only given him six months to live, however, Sammy was a fighter. He fought every day to stay with his family watching his baby girl, lil Sammy get taller and smarter by the day; he had enjoyed seeing his grandbabies have two birthdays. Alex and Alexis had recently turned two years old and he felt strong enough to walk Sincere down the aisle.

Sammy couldn't wait to see his beautiful princess on her wedding day then walk her down the aisle so she could become Mrs. Michael Saintjohn.

It's Christmas Eve 1999, Neicy and Sincere was preparing for the big Christmas Eve party they have every year at the Simmons mansion. When all the family come over, they exchanged gifts, ate good food, showed each other love and talked about all the good times they've had over the years.

Sincere is in the kitchen helping Mimi cook a few things from the evenings menu when Michael walked in and kissed her from behind, then said, "Hey, I love to see a sexy woman cooking in the kitchen; smells great baby."

Sincere blushed as she handed Michael a knife, asking him to help because she loved to see a handsome man in the kitchen. Michael laughed, but he took the knife and began chopping veggies for his future wife.

"Merry Christmas," Tyra said, walking through the door with one year old Rachael in her arms and five months pregnant with her baby boy.

Sincere hugs Tyra, then rubbed her belly saying, "I told you, you were gonna have another baby. Keep being fruitful and multiply toots, keep our family bloodline going."

Tyra popped Sincere on the butt then told her she needed to let Michael put another bun in her oven to give Alex and Alexis a playmate.

Sincere rubbed her hand across her butt then told Tyra, "No no no no more babies for me I gotta keep this ass nice and round, and this stomach nice and flat, a baby will have me out of shape with stretch marks; I pass. I love my son and daughter they are each other's playmates."

It was after midnight which officially made it Christmas day; the Simmons family were all still laughing, drinking, opening gifts and reminiscing. Sammy is holding little Samantha in his lap while she is brushing his hair with a brush that came with a doll she had gotten for Christmas.

He's looking at his wife and family thinking he never wanted to leave them. All his life he had stayed strong, working hard to make sure his family had the best of everything. If he died who

would be the rock of his family, it brought him comfort knowing Sincere had a wonderful man in Michael, what he always wanted for his baby girl.

Sitting remembering all the times he's shared with his family, Sammy got sleepy and told his wife Neicy he'd like for her to help him get into bed, he was tired and wanted to rest. Neicy helps

Sammy upstairs into his pajamas, gave him a sweet long kiss then tucks her husband into bed and goes back downstairs to see everyone off until they meet later that day for a big Christmas dinner, as they always did, however, this Christmas was going to be different from the other's; it would bring a big change to the Simmons family and Christmas would never be Christmas again.

It's 10am on Christmas morning. Sincere wakes up to Michael snoring next to her and twins sleeping sound asleep in her baby sister's room. She went in the bathroom, washed her face then headed down to her father's bedroom to wish him a Merry Christmas again. When she knocks on the door, her father doesn't say come in so she thought he's still sleeping after the long night they had with the family.

So she peeks in on him to see Sammy sound asleep and said to herself, "I'll let him rest. Mom will wake him up soon."

Sincere started to close the door back when she noticed her father's arm dangling from the bed. She walked over to place it by his side then realized her father wasn't breathing. Sincere's heart began to beat faster than it ever had before; she shook her father saying his name but he didn't reply.

She instantly tried to revive him by doing CPR, but it was too late, her father had already died. Sammy was gone. Sincere started screaming for her mom, frantically. Neicy comes running in the room to see Sincere hugging her father's lifeless body, crying. Neicy placed her hand on her before fainting because she knew the man she had shared the last 30years with was now gone forever.

The day of Sammy's funeral Sincere is staring in the mirror crying, dreading to say goodbye to her father. She had experienced pain before, but this pain she felt was different from any other pain she had felt. It felt like someone had taken a knife and repeatedly stabbed her in her heart. Her stomach was balling up, she tried to use the bathroom but couldn't. Her body hadn't stopped shaking since her father died. Her chest hurt every time she tried to take a breath. Her mother hadn't been doing well either. Neicy had been drinking nonstop, bottles and bottles of wine daily. She couldn't even focus to plan Sammy's Home going.

Sammy was all Neicy knew. She had been with him since she was fifteen. Everything she knew, Sammy taught her. Sammy had paid for her education, which led her to be the most successful black attorney in Georgia. Without Sammy, Neicy felt like her life was meaningless.

The only things that kept her going, was her two beautiful daughters who were a part of Sammy. Those girls were Sammy's pride and joy. He saw no wrong in his girls and Neicy saw no wrong in Sammy. To her, Sammy will forever be the perfect husband and father.

"Ma'am we have the limo waiting for you and your daughters outside," the nicely dressed man said, from *JEFFERY MARKS FUNERAL HOME*.

Neicy dressed in all black with a big brimmed hat and shades, looked at Sincere, who is holding on to Michael with her head down, then said, "Come on baby girl, let's go say our last goodbyes to your father."

Arriving at *CLEARY WELL FAITH CHURCH,* Michael is overwhelmed at how many people were there to show their respects to Samuel Simmons.

The line to enter the church was two miles long. People had come from all over the United States to attend the home going for Samuel Simmons.

Hugging Sincere in the back of the limo Michael said softly, "Wow baby your father was a great man who was loved by many. It had to be over two thousand people here."Not looking up to see neither the line nor the people, Sincere replied, "Yeah my father was one of a kind. He will truly be missed by many but no one will miss him more than my mother, sister, and I. The man that would move a mountain for us if he could, is now gone. I'll never hear my daddy call me baby girl anymore. I won't get his sweet kiss on the forehead. They are now just a memory. This is the hardest thing I have ever had to do. I'm gonna have to say goodbye to my father forever."

Walking into *CLEARY WELL FAITH CHURCH* the funeral director from *JEFFERY MARKS FUNERAL HOME* helps Neicy down the aisle, while she followed Pastor Willie Jackson who's reading a verse out the bible, as he guided the family to view the body of their beloved Sammy. Neicy is so shaken up when she got up to Sammy's casket, it had just hit her again that her husband, her rock, her everything, was lying in a casket never to walk in their door again. Neicy falls out and had to be taken out of the church.

Sincere shaking, Michael holding her up, kissed her father as she saw him lying there not moving, in his favorite gray Versace suit. Still handsome as ever, she just wished she could see her father's eyes one last time.

As she sat down wiping the tears from her eyes Pastor Willie Jackson asked a short heavy set woman with a short haircut to come sing Sammy's favorite gospel song, "I Won't Complain." One reason is because Sammy never once complained about his sickness or his dying; he just lived each day to the fullest.

After the funeral, Sincere saw what Michael was saying when they arrived at the church there was thousands of people surrounding the church. Sincere was seeing faces she hadn't seen in years and it seemed like everyone who purchased a car from her father paid their respects as well.

Her father had a wonderful home going and she was pleased to know he was loved so much by so many. On her way to the car so they could go to the gravesite to say their final goodbye to her father, Sincere looked up to see Konia Miles, the woman that worked for her father. The same woman she had seen her father with that night at the *LOEWS HOTEL*, but Konia wasn't alone, she had a little boy in her arms that looked around one year old or so.

Sincere turned away from the limo to go speak to Konia and to take a look at this curly haired little boy she was holding. Sincere was trying to get through the crowd to reach Konia, but everyone kept stopping her in her tracks to give their condolences and hugs.

By the time she got to Konia she had already gotten in her car and driven off. Sincere turned back around to get in the limo where her mother and Michael were waiting. As she got closer to the limo, she's thinking how much the curly haired little boy Konia was holding looked a lot like her father, but Sincere knew it couldn't be her father's child, her father would never make a baby outside of his marriage… never.

Sincere got the thought out her head as they drive to the cemetery; however, she's hoping to run into Konia again at the cemetery. But when they got to the cemetery Konia wasn't there. Sincere took that as a sign she was correct, the little boy Konia Miles was holding at her father's funeral was not her father's.

It's the year 2000; the year Sincere and Michael will be getting married. It's been three weeks since Samuel Simmons was laid to rest, the few weeks hadn't been easy for Neicy and her girls, but they were moving on.

Leaning on God to get them through the pain they were enduring. They missed Sammy more than any words could express, however, they knew he wouldn't want them to stop living their lives because his ended. Sincere was helping Neicy pack up her father's things, so they could give them away.

Michael was in the kitchen preparing dinner for them to enjoy because they haven't eaten a home cooked meal since Sammy died. Mimi was in the playroom playing with the kids.

When the doorbell rang, Little Sami comes running out the playroom saying, "Daddy, Daddy! Momma I think daddy's home now," Sami was only 6 years old, she didn't really understand that her father wasn't coming home and heaven wasn't just one of his business trips.

Mimi scooted Sami aside before opening and said, "No Sami baby, it's not your father. Your father won't be coming home today either sweetheart."

Sami crossing her arms and poking out her bottom lip said, "It's not fair, I miss daddy. When is he coming home from heaven, He's never gone this long?"

Neicy walked down the hall, calling Sami, telling her to come here. When Sami reached Neicy, she picked her up and just held her while Mimi answered the door. When Mimi answered the door, its Konia Miles standing there.

Mimi not knowing who Konia is asked," May I help you ma'am?"

Brushing her hair to the side with her fingers, Konia replied, "Yes you can, is Mrs. Neicy Simmons home?" Opening the door so she could come in, Mimi asked Konia to wait there, she would return with Mrs. Simmons.

"Mrs. Simmons, you have a lady visitor, she's in the foyer waiting for you," Neicy asked Little Sami to get down off her lap while she went see who the visitor was.

She got to the foyer there was no woman there but a small child sleeping buckled in his car seat with a letter attached to him saying, "Dear Mrs. Neicy Simmons, my name is Konia Miles. I worked for your husband many years at the dealership in California. You're probably wondering why I'm leaving you this letter attached to my son. First let me tell you his name is Kaleb Cameron Miles. He turned one year old on November eighteenth. He belongs to Sammy. Before you get upset, let me explain to you. Sammy never knew about Kaleb, I never told him, I was too ashamed because Kaleb was conceived during a one night stand. One evening after too many drinks during a business meeting, I could never bring myself to tell Sammy because I knew how he felt about you and his girls; he wanted nothing coming between him and his family's happiness. Please take care of my baby. I know I'm not fit to be the mother he needs; however, I know you are. He is such a good baby. You're going to love him. Yes I said, you're going to love him. I'm giving you full custody of him. He now belongs to you. You now have a son, Sammy's son."

Neicy dropped the letter, took Kaleb out the car seat and holds him close. When Kaleb feels Neicy's heartbeat against his, he wakes and gave Neicy a big smile. He didn't shed a tear, because he was in a stranger's arms. He felt safe and loved with Neicy.

Neicy looked into Kaleb's grey eyes and she saw her Sammy. She knew she should be upset, but she wasn't. She was happy. She believed God had sent her the son Sammy wanted them to have together. Whether she birthed Kaleb or not, he was a part of the man she loved for thirty years, and she was going to love and raise Kaleb as if he were her own.

Sincere walked from packing her father's things and saw her mother holding the curly haired little boy she had seen Konia holding at her father's funeral.

She looked at her mom and asked, "Mom, whose baby are you holding?"

Neicy kissed Kaleb, looked up at her oldest daughter then answered, "Mine baby girl, he's mine."

Chapter 25

HAPPILY EVER AFTER

Its April 1, 2000, a nice spring night in Atlanta and also the night of Sincere's bachelorette party. She was excited to see what Shay had planned. She knew it would be a night she would never forget.

Sincere is getting ready for girls night while Shay is on the phone with the entertainment for the evening making sure they would arrive on time. After the man on the phone reassured her male dancers will be there, Shay hung up the phone then helps Sincere with the Bride's sash and veil. Shay is smiling looking at Sincere in her yellow Dolce and Gabana dress. Thinking how beautiful she looked and it wasn't even her wedding day. She knew Sincere would be a beautiful bride in ten short days.

While Shay is helping Sincere fix her hair and veil, the phone rings. Shay hands the phone to Sincere without answering it, Sincere looked at the caller ID to see it was Vincent Hightower calling.

She answered "Hello Vincent, I'm glad you called. I've been meaning to return your call, but it had been rough for me these last few months and with my wedding just ten days away, I'm running around like a chicken with its head cut off."

Pausing for a moment before he said anything, Vincent was heartbroken when he heard Sincere would be married in ten days. He was hoping, seeing her after all that time at Kevin's funeral was a sign that they were meant to be together. But his hope was now crushed.

Trying to sound happy about her wedding, Vincent

said, "Married, wow Sin baby, that's wonderful news. Sure hope I can get an invite."

Sincere gave Vincent a fast, of course you're invited, and then the two make plans to have a friendly lunch to catch up on old times before Sincere got hitched. Sincere comes down the stairs to join the fourteen ladies there celebrating her soon to be marriage.

She saw head lights flashing so she took a peek out a small window and saw a long white limo pulling up. She's wondering who it could be because all the ladies were there already and Shay said the male dancers weren't coming for another hour. She's standing at the window waiting to see who was in the limo, then four nicely built men hop out of the limo and start walking towards the door.

Sincere braces herself before opening the door because she thinking, "this must be the entertainment!"

God help me behave tonight because I already feel wetness in my panties from looking at these fine men," she opened the door and said, "Come in fellas."

The first guy walked in 5'9 with muscles on top of muscles and a tattoo that said, SNAKE across his chest. The second guy walked in 6'0 with piercings and tattoos on both of his very muscular arms; his name was SILK. The third and forth guys walk in, both 6'2 with tattoos covering their whole bodies, and all you could see when you looked down was that they were blessed in every way, shape, and form. Their names were MIDNIGHT and COBRA.

After all the men were in the house, Sincere shows them where the other ladies were waiting. When the men reached the room with the ladies, Snake asked, "Which one of you sexy ass ladies is the bride to be?" all the ladies point at Sincere, who is blushing looking at the four men like she was at Baskin Robbins.

Except she didn't have 31flavors, she had 4 delicious tantalizing flavors. Snake points at Sincere, and then moves his fingers, motioning for her to come to him. She walked over to him and the show began. Those four men tossed and turned Sincere and the other ladies every which way possible.

The ladies loved it; they were throwing dollars at the men from every direction. Atlanta was known for making it rain, however, Sincere and her girls had caused a thunder storm in that bitch.

They all were satisfied, and the men were all hundreds of dollars richer than when they came. None of the ladies was ready for the men to leave. But they still had to go to *CLUB DIAMOND* to finish off their night on the dance floor and have plenty more drinks.

The party bus had just pulled up and none of them had plans on turning in until the sun came up and they did just that; the ladies partied so hard until 6am, they all fell asleep on the party bus when the driver arrived at Sincere's; he couldn't wake neither of the women up so he parked and let the ladies sleep peacefully.

April 11, 2000, the day before Sincere and Michael's big day. Sincere could not believe she will be married in 24hours. She would be Mrs. Michael Saintjohn and the happiest woman in the State of Georgia.

Sincere and Michael had agreed not to see each other the whole day before their wedding. The next time they would see each other; she would be walking down the aisle to become Mrs. Michael Saintjohn. She loved the way it sounded, Sincere Saintjohn. It was music to her ears; she would be someone's wife and she would have a husband, something she's always wanted since she was a little girl playing Barbie.

Although she was very excited about getting married, she was still preparing to have lunch with Vincent Hightower like she had promised him. She thought a nice innocent lunch between friends wouldn't hurt anything;

besides, her wedding wasn't for another 24hours; plus she knew Vincent was a gentleman and wouldn't try anything against her will.

Vincent had Sincere meet him at a small cafe in Stone Mountain called *CHERISH Café*. A place she didn't get to much. Sincere was wealthy so she went only to upscale places in Atlanta. This would be very different for her. She walked in *CHERISH CAFE* and Vincent was waiting there at a booth. He waved so Sincere could see him sitting at the small booth in the corner. She approaches him. Vincent stands up, gave her a kiss on the cheek, and then asked her to have a seat.

The two have a nice lunch between old friends, catching up on everything that had happened in their lives since high school. Vincent told Sincere how after high school his father and mother divorced which left them broke, so he never got to attend college like he wanted, instead he ended up going to the police academy and became a police officer taking a vow to protect and serve.

Vincent took his job very seriously. He even arrested his mother at one time for an old warrant she had which was 10 years old. However, Vincent being a faithful man to his job had no choice but to take his mom in. He did bond her out to ease the anger she was feeling towards him for arresting his own mother.

Sincere is amazed and saddened by some of the things Vincent had shared with her. It made her realize how blessed she's been in her life, and thanked God for blessing her with the life she had. It hadn't been perfect, however, she’s never gone without, and she had the best of everything.

After talking awhile at *CHERISH CAFE* Vincent convinced Sincere to finish their conversation at his apartment with a cocktail. His place was only around the corner from the café. Sincere figured it wouldn't hurt anything, besides Vincent was an old friend and now a policeman. A fine policeman at that. Sincere knew she was most definitely in good hands.

Walking into his small apartment, Sincere is looking around, she thought to herself, "Wow, so this how the other half lives. This apartment is the size of my family room, but I guess it's not where you live, it's what you make of it." Smiling at Vincent, Sincere asked, "So Mr. Hightower, where's that cocktail you promised me, I sure could use it right about now," walking over to his small bar.

Vincent began pouring him and Sincere a drink. He pours Sincere a glass of Alize with a splash of orange juice, then pours himself a double shot of Remy. They have a seat on his sofa to share a cocktail, however, the one cocktail turned into four cocktails.

By the time Sincere was half done with her four glasses, she most definitely had a buzz going, because she began to babble. Sincere had begun telling Vincent something she had never shared with anyone except Tyra and Shay. Sincere had told Vincent how Kevin Millhouse had raped her and how she had to have an abortion at a young age. Then she explained how she never truly got over what Kevin had done to her; she still had nightmares because of it.

Vincent saw the hurt in Sincere's eyes.

He went to console her, but his consoling turned into kissing. "I'm sorry, I just couldn't help myself, you're so beautiful," Vincent said, as he's pulling away from Sincere's soft lips.

Liking what Vincent just did, Sincere pulled him back towards her and the two begin kissing passionately. Before Sincere knew it, their clothes were off and Vincent had his tongue so far up in Sincere's pussy she felt as if she was getting her monthly cleaning from him. She thought Vernon had a mean tongue, however, she was wrong. Vincent ate

Sincere's pussy so well and clean, like she had taken a bath. Vincent had her body squirting out things she never knew it could. She couldn't take it anymore.

She pushed Vincent's head from in between her legs, and then said, "Lay your ass down on this couch. I'm about to fuck the hell out of you. You're about to feel the softest place on earth, I hope you're ready."

She took Vincent's very thick 10inch penis, placed it where She knew he wanted it to be. She began moving her hips.

Vincent, rolling the back of his head, started grabbing Sincere's ass saying, "Oh my god Sin, this pussy is everything I'd thought it would be and more mmmmmmmm, it's so good. I can stay init, forever, please don't stop, ride this big black dick, girl ride it like it's the last dick you're gonna get. Fuck me baby," the more Vincent talked the harder Sincere rode his big black dick, as he called it. Sincere had just made Vincent lose his mind.

When she rose up from him, he pulled her back down and whispered, "Don't leave, I want to feel you all night. I never had a woman squeeze my dick so hard with her muscles and work me the way you just did. Please let me have some more?"

She licked her lips at Vincent, then turned around lifted her ass in the air and told Vincent come and get it if you want it. Vincent's dick got rock hard. He rammed it in Sincere. She loved it. She's begging Vincent to fuck her harder until he makes her pussy explode her juices all over his dick.

Vincent gave Sincere what she asked for and when her pussy exploded, Vincent fell under Sincere's spell, he was just like the rest. One dose and now he was hooked, but Sincere would be married tomorrow so she had to leave Vincent lying on the couch, dying for another dose of her love.

Walking out his apartment door, she thought to herself, "That was a wonderful way to end my last day of being Sincere Simmons," and walked to her car." "Mommy's getting married today," Sincere said, to the twins as she's combing Alexis's hair for the wedding.

"Yaaaaaay Mommie," Alex and Alexis said, back clapping their hands.

Annabelle walked in the room with two sippy cups for the twins, then said to Sincere in her heavy accent, "I'm very happy for you, Mrs. Simmons, however, I'm going to miss working for you; I've become attached to you and your children."

Sincere stops running the brush through Alexis's long thick curly hair, hugs Annabelle and lets her know she is family to her and her two children; the thought of her leaving never crossed her mind. She too was coming to live with them in *MOXLEY ESTATES*. She and Michael had already talked about it; he would keep his housekeeper and she would keep her Annabelle.

All the girls in the wedding were starting to arrive at Sincere's. The two limos would be there by noon to take them to *LIZZY'S BOTANICAL GARDEN and AQUARIUM* where Sincere and Michael's wedding ceremony and reception would be held.

Shay is looking at Sincere thinking how beautiful she looked and she's not even in her wedding gown yet. Her piercing green eyes were looking so bright, like she had diamonds in her eyes. Shay also couldn't wait for Sincere to see the surprise Michael had waiting for Sincere once they reached *LIZZY'S BOTANICAL GARDEN and AQUARIUM.*

What Sincere didn't know was Michael bought *LIZZY'S BOTANICAL GARDEN and AQUARIUM* and had work done to it so it would be everything Sincere wanted it to be. All Michael wanted was for Sincere to be happy. She was his queen and he'd do any and everything possible to make sure he was her king.

"Ladies, ladies, the limo is here," said, Momma Foster, clapping her hands together for the ladies to hurry alone. Momma Foster was the wedding coordinator for this big extravagant wedding Sincere and Michael were having.

It had been a rough two years finding everything Sincere wanted; however, Momma Foster had pulled it off. Because she too wanted the best for Sincere and her grandbabies. Lex would have wanted them well taken care of, and she knew Michael would pick up where her son left off, and if he didn't, she would make sure he would pay for any hurt he caused them.

Guests were arriving and everyone was intrigued with how beautifully the place was decorated. Every chair had a white or light pink silk cover. There were fresh cut white and pink roses everywhere. What wasn't light pink and white was blinged out. From the ceiling, hung beautiful crystal chandeliers; the aisle was long which lead to a wide staircase behind the staircase was a huge glass wall filled with ocean water that contained every tropical creature found at sea; it was breathtaking. Sincere was sure to be a very happy bride.

"Okay ladies and gentlemen line up, the organist had begun playing the song," Momma Foster said, getting the wedding party ready for the wedding.

Lining up, Shay and Tyra were the last ones in the line. So Momma Foster closed the double doors where Sincere and the flower girls were waiting. As they wait for the cue to walk down the aisle, Shay glanced over at a man standing in the far off corner as if he didn't want to be seen. Trying to focus on what she's about to do, she turned around and waited for Momma Foster to tell her to walk, right as Shay took the first step to walk down the aisle, something made her look back to see if the strange man was still standing there and he was. This time she got a good look at who he was, it was Vernon James.

About to walk down the aisle, she couldn't go up to him and slap the hell out of him then ask the two questions she wanted to know, #1 Why the hell are you here and #2 Why the hell did he beat her friend to hell like that?

The wedding party is all down the aisle the ladies are in their light pink chiffon dress with their blinged out jewelry and glass heels. The men all stood there tall and handsome with their white tux's accented in light pink.

Michael and Pastor Willie Jackson are standing their waiting for his bride. The flower girls, little Sami and 2year old Alex looked so darling coming down the aisle, throwing little crystals that looked like diamonds instead of flowers; the guests at the wedding just adored the two precious angels walking down the aisle.

The church was silent, then all of a sudden 2year old Alex comes rushing down the aisle in his white tux, yelling in his little voice, "MY MOMMIES COMING, MY MOMMIES COMING," all the guest laughed because he was supposed to say "THE BRIDE IS COMING, THE BRIDE IS COMING," but it was still so cute, it made a special moment in the wedding itself.

Nervous, arm to arm with her uncle Steve, Sincere started to think how she missed her father and how she wished he could be there to share her day. She tried to hold back her tears because she knew her father would want her happy on today. But some days are harder to deal with her father's death than other's and today, her wedding day would be one of those hard days; she had comfort knowing he was here in spirit, her guardian angel.

The double doors opened; all the guests stood up and out came Sincere looking amazingly gorgeous. The guest oooooed and ahhhhhhhed as her Uncle Steve escorted her down the aisle in her pure white VERA WANG custom made wedding gown that was covered in diamonds with a train that was 6ft long.

The dress was beautiful and fit her perfectly. She walked down the aisle looking like an angel; tears came from Michael's eyes, as he watched his wife to be walk towards him. He was thinking he was the luckiest man alive. Right now he was marrying a beautiful young successful woman. She was his queen and he her king; they were man and wife MR and MRS. MICHAEL SAINTJOHN.

One o'clock am and the reception was finally over. The 300 wedding guest were all gone and now Sincere and her new husband could go home and start their pre-honeymoon. Michael had decided a while ago the night of the wedding, he wanted them to spend one last night in Sincere's home before she packed up to come to their new home together in *MOXLEY ESTATES.*

When the limo pulled them into Sincere's driveway, she saw that Shay's car was parked there. Sincere thought it was strange because Shay didn't tell her she was going to spend the night, but she blew it off. She and Michael headed in the house.

They get in the house they see no sign of no one. Sincere walked around. She went in her family room where she saw Shay passed out drunk in her $1,200 maid of honor dress.

Sincere shook her head, got a blanket and covered Shay up, then said, "Drunken bitch, I love her though."

Shay heard Sincere half sleep, she opened one eye then said, "I got something I want to tell you and I didn't want to tell you while your wedding and reception was going on."

Sincere told Shay, shhhh ok you can tell me in the morning, right now sleep the alcohol off babe." Sincere then headed to her bedroom where her husband was waiting. She got to her room and didn't waste any time; she took off every piece of clothing she had on. Then beat Michael getting in the bed, Michael didn't even get part of his body in the bed before Sincere attacked him like he was a deer and she was a hungry lion. Looking to satisfy her hunger, she gave Michael the best sex he ever had; his reaction let her know he was never going anywhere; this marriage was going to be forever til Death do them part.

April 13, 2000, its 10am the day after Sincere and Michael were married. She woke up next to Michael still smiling, looking at the big 10ct diamond ring she had on her finger.

Rolling over to grab her robe, Sincere decides she'd make breakfast for everyone while they were sleeping. The smell of some pancakes, bacon, eggs, grits and biscuits should wake them up she said to herself, as she headed to the kitchen. As she pulled the things she needed out the fridge, her doorbell rings. She finished placing the stuff on the counter, and then walked down the hall to answer the door.

She figured it might be Michael's driver bringing more wedding presents over. So without seeing who it was she opened the door, standing there with tears in his eyes was Vernon James. He walked in and stands in the foyer. Sincere is in shock, because she hadn't seen Vernon since he beat her at his home. She opened her mouth to ask Vernon what was he doing there, but he stopped her then said, "Sincere baby I'm sorry I never meant to hurt you. I love you. I've learned from what I did to you. I'll never do it again baby, please take me back."

As Vernon standing there waiting for an answer, Shay comes walking down the hall rubbing her eyes, asking Vernon, "What the hell was he doing here. Sincere is married," before Vernon could answer Shay, Sincere's doorbell rings again running her fingers through her hair wondering who else could be trying to ruin her morning;

she opened the door and standing there was Vincent Hightower and beside him were four other Atlanta policeman.

Sincere is standing there looking confused at Vincent. Vincent looked at her then said, "Sin baby don't worry I'm going to get you out of this."

Sincere looked at Shay who motions her mouth saying, "Remember what I told you, you didn't do anything."

Sincere is standing in her doorway scared not knowing what's going to happen when the tall freckled face policeman next to Vernon said, "Ma'am are you Sincere Sunshine Simmons? We need you to come down to the station for questioning about the murder of Kevin Millhouse."

Sincere put her head down in disbelief, and then said to herself, "Damn, which way is my life going to take me now."

The End

Bio – Shanika “Neek” Washington 2012

How is greatness defined? New Author Shanika “Neek” Washington expresses her storied life through her writing. The first time author of “Sincere’s Ways” pours her heart into what she shows as raw and riveting. Born December 7, 1976 in Rockford, IL, Neek, as her fans and followers address her, now resides in Atlanta, GA.

After completing high school in 1995 and diving into a study of early childhood development, Mrs. Washington found treasure in motherhood. She is a wife, and mother. Even tried her hand as a sales consultant in the telecommunications industry, before settling on Direct Care Taking for the elderly and mentally challenged.

In Sincere’s Ways, readers are pulled into what life is like in modern day Atlanta, GA through the eyes of the main character. Everyone has heard of how Sister Souljah’s “The Coldest Winter Ever” transcended pop culture and brought the mean, inner city streets to life with the triumph of a young girl; well, here we go again. Sincere’s Ways has the power of making Mrs. Washington a household name and the story she describes, majestic!

www.ingramcontent.com/pod-product-compliance
Lightning Source LLC
Chambersburg PA
CBHW070825180626
46818CB00001B/403
* 9 7 8 0 5 7 8 1 1 7 0 9 6 *